# THE VILLAGE CURTAIN

## CURTAIN

## TONY TAME

Savant Books
Honolulu, HI, USA
2009

Published in the USA by Savant Books and Publications
2630 Kapiolani Blvd #1601
Honolulu, HI 96826
http://www.savantbooksandpublications.com

Printed in the USA

Edited by Tara Dine
Cover photograph courtesy of Mr. Richard Khouri, O.D.

ISBN: 0-9841175-0-4
EAN-13: 978-0-9841175-0-5

# DEDICATION AND ACKNOWLEDGEMENT

To my wife Jennifer and daughter Stephanie, who never wavered in their faith and belief that these stories should be told. To Tara Dine who undertook the painstaking task of pointing out to me that punctuation ought to be included, and to the many fishermen of Jamaica with whom I have worked and whose voices are seldom heard.

# TABLE OF CONTENTS

# PART 1

# KINGFISH SEASON

All year long, big kingfish range east and west along the deep drop-offs from Morant Point on the eastern tip of Jamaica to the offshore banks south of Black River and Bluefields. Twice a year, they move very close to land over the shallow water of the fringing reef. It must have something to do with the reproductive cycle of the animal, as all of the females are heavy with roe when this occurs. They feed with enthusiasm, as do many fish at that time of their lives, provided they are not a species that die after spawning. The only thing that gives fishermen a problem is that the kingfish concentrate for this feeding frenzy in the very first light. So it comes down, as it so often does, to taking advantage of biting times if you hunt speed-loving, predatory creatures with a liking for a really early breakfast.

Actually they start a little before the sunlight is properly established, when the sun is just a promise and the sea is only a darker—though white-flecked—patch than the paler grey-black of the horizon. February is one of the harvest times; a month of whistling northeast winds. These winds drive broad, anvil clouds with frayed and shredded heads; their manes pulled and torn away, strung out threadlike and streaking above the crack-of-dawn sky, so there is that to contend with as well. Consequently, there is less illumination than you would get on a clear, calm summer morning. It looks positively northern hemisphere, like an English Channel type of setting, but a bit warmer.

Of course temperature is a relative thing. A man used to hauling king crab traps in proximity to the polar seas would laugh at the idea of being cold if you were situated a scant seventeen degrees north of the equator, but early morning spray with a twenty-five mile per hour breeze behind it and the same old abrasive, eye singeing salt as they have all over the world's oceans is no picnic either. The boats these old boys use are only fifteen to eighteen feet long, wide open, and have an engine that has been battering away at this trade for twice the time that its designer ever intended as a reasonable life expectancy—if the thing was used on a civilized Canadian lake.

A visiting engineer from the Johnson and Evinrude factory once asked, "What on God's earth is that?" when brought face to face with one of these relics.

"It's really an anchor," the fisherman said, "but we pretend it's a motor."

These old, well-loved machines sound pretty rough when you start them in the tiny harbor, but the noise would be even worse if the big wind didn't whip most of it away. In any case, after a few minutes all the uneven clattering of bearings and varying vibrations from broken rubber mounts are lost completely in the hiss and crash of breaking waves. The semi-flat hull also makes an impressive noise after it comes off the top of a six-foot swell and falls straight down through the empty air onto the confused surface of the next trough.

Long ago, a few of these boats would split doing that free fall routine but the miracle of fiberglass matting, stretched and glued to the wooden hulls, has generally stopped such embarrassment—except when the job is rushed or done with insufficient finances to ensure the proper adhesion of this wonder skin. In that unfortunate event you get situations where the coating separates suddenly and peels back, only to wind itself up in the propeller leaving you powerless in more ways than one. If that happens very close to the reef then this whole merchant marine investment, not to mention the investor, is going to get liquidated in a minute or two unless he can get an anchor overboard and holding well. So if there exists any doubt about the integrity of the boat's bottom, it is advisable to keep a close and intense watch on the whole situation below the water line. You can tell the fellows with the least cash and confidence because they spend a lot of time poking around underneath their craft with little knives.

If you are already broke when this brief kingfish season comes along and you notice bubbles and cracks in the fiberglass, what do you do precisely? You go out and catch some of these profitable fish to buy what you need or stay safe inside and watch the shell erode and strip away until it gets to where you might never catch up with the cost of the material required (which is petroleum-based, as they say, and getting more costly by the day).

So you keep a little further off the grinning, spitting coral teeth and plan on using that precious seaway margin as an area of maneuver, while trying to shield the little boat as much as you can by quartering the sea and cutting power when the truly awful waves roll in. You use all the old tricks that men in dicey vessels have employed against foul weather, along with prayers and hope, although you know quite well that doing all these things will handicap you in making the best catch and, in the end, you just wish silently and secretly for the

fisherman's real, and only, friend: luck. This is
done covertly because talking confirms weakness at sea.
We're supposed to be strong and silent types who inspire
confidence in the two man crew, who already knows how
bad it is and are doing all they can not to comment as per
the same macho rule of maritime *omerta*.

But let's assume you are in a boat that is fairly
well connected and powered by something built at least
during the last twenty years and conditions are no worse
than the usual chilly February daybreak. You have out
two hand lines, one shorter than the other to avoid a
tangle. You hook the first fish as you clear the channel
and, a few seconds later, another one takes it while the
first is still out there trying to shake free, mix up the lines,
break away or get off anyway it can. On top of all that,
you also have to keep out of the way of other boats all
around you that might be fighting fish of their own. It can
be awfully hectic on a good morning and everybody has
to work swiftly and cooperatively and try not to fall
overboard or do anything stupid or expensive because

this is all about making some quick money, particularly now with the light getting brighter all the time. It's a race with the light. Once the sun gets well clear of the day-clouds and the rays begin to shift from horizontal to just a bit more vertical, the whole school of big, silver-grey, pointy toothed predators with voracious appetites is going to sink away to who knows where. After that you are lucky to catch one in an hour, where you previously put ten aboard in thirty minutes.

In a good season, you will have one week of this action either side of the full moon and that's it. You will have lots of time after that to grumble at the fisherman's lot and spend what was earned in that interlude trying to keep the old tub seaworthy. Not to mention listening to how, in your great-grandfather's day, the kingfish came right inside the little bay. Imagine, right over the clear sand and weed patches. Men in rowboats caught four hundred pounds of them in broad daylight. It must be true because everybody says so. The wind must have been much lighter back then, how else could they row into it?

Perhaps they had muscles as big as their catches. Maybe it was possible, especially if they didn't have to go outside the harbor. Just think of how many fish there must have been if you could still find them feeding at midday.

It's getting harder all the time.

"It must be global warming," said one of the younger ones. This one listens to the radio all the time.

"Did it feel warm out there this morning?"

"Not really." Christ Almighty! It felt like it could've blown the teeth out of a handsaw. It goes right through you.

Funnily enough, you can sweat secretly in the crisp air of the early morning underneath the spray of the chilly salt water. The really big combers, rearing up with their crests ripped off backward by the force of the rushing wind as they race toward you, will make you do that. The way you deal with these water mountains is to not focus on how they look, unless you are the helmsman, who must pay attention and decide quickly how to deal with each and every one. That's why the owner drives the boat. He has everything to lose and is too busy to sweat. And this whole sweating business is another one of the unmentionables, at least among the initiated tribal members.

During the time of year that passes for the tropical winter, the sea wind drops away in the late afternoon and the foam line growling on the reef gradually falls out until it is just locatable by the muffled, mumbly grumble. As the night comes on quickly and completely, the land breeze steals the cool, wet-plant scent off the flanks of the Blue Mountains. The beachfront water surface turns silky for a few hours, smoothed by the reverse flow of the wind. Soon, the ancient forces of wind and tide will ally themselves with the creatures of the sea once again. A sensible fisherman would try to get one more hour of rest before he takes another shot at the old duel but, down by the shoreline, the first ominously confident salty breaths of the open ocean tempest puff again. The roar arises once more and outside, beyond the rocky ramparts in the field of combat, the next morning's modern version of ancient jousting for dollars and reputation will start again until the moon phase calls it quits absolutely. That is when everybody goes back to discussing full time how it was in our ancestors' days when the fish patrolled close along the shore. Now the children play, growing up as fast as they can, impatient to take their turn at the game.

The Charity Man came and had a really good look at all of this nonsense. He held this title not because he was a recipient of alms but rather because he was a dispenser of them. The Charity Man was attached to a worldwide movement engaged in the spreading of good works and handouts abroad and he walked the highways and byways doing good to the less fortunate among us. He was an intelligent man, and no starry eyed do-gooder, so he understood quickly and totally the frightful inefficiency and faintly desperate nature of what was going on.

He came two weeks after the season was over and four of the six boats were still in the beach hospital undergoing tightening operations as vital to them as face-lifts are said to be for the Hollywood elite. Without these procedures they would never be able to go, with even the slightest confidence, eye to eye with their ancient adversary. Every engine was in some stage of recovery, some getting transplants from dead relatives found at motor graveyards in more progressive communities, where people understood that what you did with junk was throw it away.

The Charity Man observed a propeller being pinned. When they make propellers, their blades are built separately from the center, or hub, and the blade assembly is forced over the hub by a hydraulic press. When age, general abuse, and ungoverned racing between wave crests causes this bond to fail, you get a new propeller. Or you pin it. Pinning is accomplished by drilling a hole through the blade base straight into the hub and fastening them solidly with a bolt. It won't slip now, or ever again, unless the bolt breaks. You think they don't know that at the factory? They do, but they also know that the rubber interface between the outside and the splined center that fits over the propeller shaft is there to give just a little slip, like a flexible coupling, so that the impact of taking up the strain is eased enough to relieve the pressure on the teeth of the gears and the engagement shock to the clutch. It's not just some first world conspiracy to sell propellers.

So when you pin a prop you get away with exchanging the price of a whole kingfish for a new propeller but, down the road, you're looking at maybe a whole gear case rebuild and that is totally out of the question. So you'll have to scour the island for an old, discarded lower unit, with suspect gears inside it at best, but it might not happen this year. Who knows for sure how faithful tired, worn-out steel may be? Good luck is always knocking around somewhere. The owners are aware of this potential pinning problem but they know just as well that this season was no record breaker. Just barely average.

A new propeller for each of the engines would be

a nice charitable gesture. In fact, six new engines or, better yet, six new boats *with* engines would be just fine, thought The Charity Man. "I'm going to see if I can get some help for you," he told the respectful group assembled around him. He tried to sound confident although he knew how it went at his evangelical organization.

One man spoke up. "You think you can arrange some money? We know what we need to buy. Every man know what him need to get."

"Let me see what I can do," said The Charity Man. He had been to many beach meetings and knew the dangers of sudden changes in social atmosphere. Long ago he tried to explain the limitations of his organization at gatherings, which had seemed quite friendly at the start, only to find that he had been forced to beat a hasty retreat. It only took one or two members of the group saying, "You sound like one politician," until suddenly you had the first bottle thrown at you. Modern politicians on the island had discovered this also and, they too, had developed the art of skirting the truth rather than admitting the inability to perform miracles.

This individual type of fishing did not get a lot of approval back home where The Charity Man's board of directors sat. The idea was cooperation, group activity, and pulling together to share in the Christian spirit. The Charity Man could get funds for a fairly big boat that would help a whole village but this diminutive outpost didn't even have a safe channel to get in and out. The whole thing has to make sense, at least sustain itself, or people think you don't care what is done with the donations. This entire small boat shoestring operation, working out of some hole on the southeast tip of the coast, can't even afford a few propellers. Anything you give them is throwing good money after bad.

But this kingfish thing is interesting because they must be around all the time. Where do they go when they move out? Now that's something we can get real funds to find out about. Then, maybe, you can do something to help the whole island.

The plan got bigger. A Florida ex-kingfish netter, before they banned such methods up there, offered to sell The Charity Man's foundation his now useless boat and equipment and throw in six months tuition to show Jamaicans what drifting gill nets could produce. It gets to be run out of Kingston, naturally, because that's where the marketing is and it's on the doorstep of the government fishing administration headquarters so you get to keep proper records. The idea is to cut the prey off in clear, open water. No fooling around with this coral head and snaggy bottom ignorance. It works well. And they *are* there all year. They just move about a bit.

The south coast of the island is roughly one hundred fifty miles long but it's not the whole length that you have to cover. Proper research reveals that it's just four pockets where kingfish retreat and so we can sock it to them good because we've really got their number now. Twenty miles of netting all put together and this is good tackle. It certainly did an absolutely marvelous job when it was working from the Carolinas all the way to Key

West. In the heyday of that fishery they were grinding up half the catch for fertilizer because they couldn't sell them all to the smokehouses. Fished properly, it will take about three years before this killing machine gets non-viable and, anyway, there are some of these pesky conservationists poking around now. There was even an article written by The Charity Man, now retired, complaining about some of the projects as though he wasn't part of it himself. He was something of a hesitant type even back then. Always was a bit suspect as a team player.

Twenty miles away along the coast they were getting the ballroom of the Convention Hotel ready for a seminar on "Sustainability in Caribbean Fisheries" which was to be hosted by the Ministry of Agriculture and Fisheries who could just scrape together enough money for that sort of get-together but damn little else. The guest speaker was from abroad, which meant that he must be an expert in the big picture. Must be. The card said he was a PhD from Norway, which was where they invented that harpoon gun that fires a shaft that goes right inside a whale and then explodes. These seafarers of Northern Europe were so wonderful and efficient. His address was to be on marine resource sustainability.

The introductory speech would be given by the Director of Fisheries who, being far from a fool, knew a lot about how conditions really were but did his best to keep his department in an atmosphere of sustainability itself. After all, if you got to a point where you had to admit that there was no viable fishing industry at all, the awkward question might arise as to what we should do with the Fisheries Division.

So everybody was assembled in the spirit of sustainability. This would be such a valuable contribution and the participants were looking forward to discussing the keynote address, complete with brilliant similes, that this distinguished foreign personage would give. So instructive. And everybody needs a job in these tough times.

Back in the village, they don't have to risk life and limb in that February maelstrom anymore. Only one boat is still up there and it is a rowboat whose weathered owner sets a few wire mesh fish traps just outside the bay for the few spiny lobster and bottom feeders that have always been there. Just four families still live around the crescent of the beach. They have built themselves a discrete, curtained existence around a new reality.

Every now and then, a well-dressed man in a Land Rover comes by to check on these people. He stops his vehicle where the road ends and honks his horn. The community watchman goes up to the driver's window as it slides open and they whisper.

"Nothing special going down?"

"No, Boss. Quiet as usual."

"Stay indoors tonight," says the driver as he hands over some very welcome cash. "Take care of everybody."

Later, from their bedrooms, the villagers might hear the smooth, powerful sound of twin eight-cylinder inboard engines carried inland by the indiscrete wind and the little murmur of a dingy motor betrays where the boys are working on the pick-up and, in the morning, quite a few debts are paid off at various stores in the town of Morant Bay and some new credit is arranged. These transactions are carried out with smaller, owner-managed shops where they understand these things. Their prices are higher than at the big business establishments but everybody knows that is because they all have to wait on the Land Rover man and he comes when he is good and ready. That's why those four families hang on like a bunch of owls. Just keeping an eye on the surroundings year round is steady work, in a way. It takes patience but that's okay because there aren't any lively young folk among them who would find this boring.

Coming back from hauling the traps, old Lester was dragging his baited line as usual behind his boat with the single tattered sail in the hope of catching a mackerel or a small barracuda. It was eleven in the morning and as clear and blazing bright as you could imagine with just enough breeze to fill his multi-patched sail. He was over that clear sand bottom with the weed patches and he damn near got pulled right over the transom from the shock and power of the strike, but he's a tough old guy and still using one of the heavy lines from back when he had the motor and trolled outside, so he hung on. The kingfish had to fight the boat itself, pulling back against the dead weight, and when Lester got him he weighed fifty-two pounds. Now even if you knock about five or six pounds off that, for we all know Lester's scale is adjusted to squeeze a few extra cents out of the buyer, that's a mighty fine fellow, a great-grandfather type of fish. Just consider that! A kingfish patrolling right alongside the shore where the children used to play!

# THE DAY BEFORE

Navigation Aids: Port Authority of Jamaica (Extract)

Lovers Leap Light Position: 17 51' 42.5" N, 77 39' 37" W

Characteristic: White Flash

Height: 1,750 ft.

Range of Visibility: 40+ miles

Structure: White, round tower, red bands

Note: One of the ten highest elevated lighthouse structures located in the Western Hemisphere. People love to visit this very high point overlooking a spectacular, sheer descent to the sea. They sometimes get a chance to stand on the edge and observe small aircraft *flying below them* as these planes traverse the coastline. People with weak stomachs and height aversion might wish to wait in their cars.

The lighthouse timer still had a while to go before it turned on the sweeping beam when Allan came in through the only door in the two roomed house and said,

"Can you believe this weather?"

"Is it too pretty to last, you think?"

"No. There is no sound at all in the waves. Smoothed right out. Two days more at least. Maybe more but not less."

"Well," Myra said, "That's enough then."

The late afternoon light was going fast and only the flaming western sky had any real illumination left. Inside the house it was dark. He tried to relax but it was not so easy. *Think about afterwards. That's how to handle it.* As a boy he had been a top sprinter in the village and when they had contests he always thought about how he was going to feel after he won and it was the best way to cool down the nervousness.

"You got a price on the new engine?"

"Yes," she said. "Mr. James called them for me. It's a fortune. A quarter million dollars. Our dollar is a joke nowadays."

"That's about three thousand and a bit American money. That won't be a problem."

*And now the weather is no problem either,* Myra thought. *There aren't any problems at all.* She didn't say it because she knew that you could do lots of damage by talking about something like that. Her own mother had come home one night after a ride back from Kingston on the venerable Field Marshall bus, which had taken more than seven miserable, boiling, dust-choked hours. The creaky old vehicle had broken down every few miles and all the passengers had to get out and, sometimes, take everything off because twice they had to raise the thing up and do mysterious stuff underneath which required lots of loud cursing. The decrepit jack couldn't lift the weight with all the boxes and cases aboard. Eventually, everybody had started saying highly insulting things to the driver when he had to stop and he would reply, "You think me want to drive this thing? Any of you want to drive it? Come drive it if you think you is better than me or keep yourselves quiet!"

When her mother got home she looked like she was hardly able to make it as far as the bed. "How you feel, Ma?"

Her mother, who was only sixty, or so she claimed, answered, "Me fine. There's nothing wrong with me. You going to be tired of seeing me around. Me going to live to be one hundred and plus like your great-granny. That's something me know for sure." But her mother had gone right to sleep after that and she never woke up. So, from then on, Myra never spoke about successful ventures yet to evolve or commented confidently upon desired outcomes, but she thought about them turning out that way all the time and it did not seem to do anything particularly harmful so she had become a mental optimist.

She looked at Allan and thought, *Me going to have you with me forever.* That idea was so optimistic that she shivered at even thinking it. You have to be careful even having thoughts like that. People sometimes say their thoughts aloud in their sleep and she wondered if that would count. That would seem unfair but, then, life is.

The lighthouse came on and the rotating flash of the screened light whirled past the window. It was official recognition proclaiming the arrival of the night.

"Me going to get the lantern going," she said. Her old dog came in through the door while she was pumping up the pressure valve on the Tilley lamp. He was a formal sort of dog and basically respected the judgment of the lighthouse when it came to things like announcements concerning the end of the day. After the big hurricane, the beacon had quit signaling for more than a month and he had regarded it as most unsettling. Like many residents of Jamaica, he had gradually come to harbor a suspicion about things maintained by the government but he still had some respect for them. A dog ought to be able to count on some regularity in his environment. He was quite certain that he would have Allan and Myra with him forever, sure that they were more reliable than the lighthouse, which had let him down badly on the occasion when it failed.

Myra gave the dog a shiny, well-gnawed ox-tail

27

bone. "Here you go," she said. "Here's your toothbrush."

Allan looked at the two of them and thought, *Jesus—me so lucky*. But, having picked up the habit of caution about saying that type of thing, he just hung the hissing lantern on a nail and said, "In the morning no come down to the boat with me when me leaving. It wouldn't be normal and the most important thing is that everything must look normal. After we go you find out from Mr. James if him can ask the vendor to bring his big van tomorrow night. Tell him me going to haul all the pots—not just one set—and me expect to make a good catch."

Every fisherman always expects that. You can't be a pessimist if you rely on the sea to keep you alive.

# DAYBREAK

The two beach walkers stopped for a while and watched as a brightly painted canoe with a yellow bow cap headed out from the curving bay. The sound of the slightly rough-running engine was the only audible noise in the exceptionally quiet morning. Not even the usual murmur of the beach surf was noticeable in the breathless air. The man was pleased at the pause. He had come to understand why they condition horses by running them on sand. As the trainers of these animals say, it challenges the tendons.

"Just you take a look at that," he said. "Can you imagine? There's a man going off to work. You think he has even the faintest idea how lucky he is?"

"Why not?" the woman said. "Maybe every night he says, 'God, look how fortunate I am.' "

"I bet he doesn't. People never know when they're ahead of the game. I bet all he does is grumble about the price of gas, or what he gets for his fish in that lunatic currency they have, or how his wife can't cook or something."

"Boy, does that sound familiar."

"No, but seriously Sonia. If I had that kind of freedom I would know better than to bitch about little things. Even this holiday only makes it more awful to go home." He looked down and began kicking at the sand. "Do you have any idea what my desk is going to look like tomorrow? I spend all of my time arguing with bureaucrats about permits, zoning infringements, and parking space. If I do ten minutes design it takes six weeks to get a department flunky to decide if my parabolic roof is going to block light out of some pigeon nest."

Sonia made no immediate comment having heard that, and the other wonderful verbal embroidery work on similar themes, hundreds of times. Privately, she was not overly enthusiastic about going back to their apartment either. Their apartment was in a city where the local authorities posted daily notices about air quality so that the population could somehow be expected to prepare itself for that particular blend of suspended particles and gas combinations that would have to be ingested for the next twenty-four hours. But she was used to being the voice of reason so she finally rose to the occasion.

"Well Robert, think about coming down here then. You can build something for them that might be a bit more comfortable than those shacks up there." She pointed at the diminutive houses and huts dotting the hillside around and above the fishing beach. Realizing that this was a nice point, she continued, "And while you're doing that you can live in one of those home-sweet-native-homes to really get the feel of how lucky these folks are. Then you can truly appreciate the nuances of the weather when a lot of it gets right inside with you. And the wildlife, you know. Different insects flying around your head at different times of the day so you don't even need a watch. One type for early morning— like these that are biting the hell out of me right now— another kind that sting at midday and then the evening shift mosquitoes, midnight scorpions and so on. Imagine how lucky you're going to feel. Not like the big fury you get into if something happens to the air conditioning thermostat at home or like the time the pipes froze and you said that nobody ought to live more than twenty degrees away from the equator. All those little insignificant difficulties will be a thing of the past. You'll just have to keep an eye out for crocodiles and black widow spiders."

The canoe was now far out on the silver-plated sea.

The man took one more look at it and said, "Let's head back to the hotel. They should have breakfast ready by now. They sure charge enough."

"Go on ahead," Sonia said. "I'm just going to walk to where they haul up the boats."

Sonia continued down the beach, thinking about what had happened just a few days ago. While they were driving the coast road from Black River to Kingston and had just left the outskirts of town, Robert spotted a woman walking along the roadside. She was carrying a bag that looked heavy and he had pulled over to offer her a lift. It was the kind of thing he did instinctively. For all his disillusionments and personal love of constant complaining, he was the kindest and most considerate man Sonia had ever known and she always prized that in his nature.

The woman got in and thanked them with a smile as wide and white and warm as the curving coral-sand beach that bordered the highway. A perfect example of the "country woman" as the more sophisticated Kingston dwellers would have called her with slight distain. Solidly built; a body that had started to get acquainted with hard work from the time it could walk but was never deprived of food in generous portions. She was wearing a little necklace with a silver "M" charm that sparkled in the sun. The woman asked to be dropped at the next village. That was only about five miles away.

Robert stopped the car where she indicated and they watched as a young man stepped out from under the porch of the little roadside bar. Seeing him, the woman gave her remarkable smile and called out, "Come here! Take this bag, Allan!" The shopping bag had overturned in the car and a few rolls of duct tape had spilled out on the floor. The man waited long enough for her to thank us formally for the ride and, standing beside her, had waved to us as Robert drove off slowly. Both of them waved.

*I have this picture of them so perfectly in my mind that I could draw it, if I could draw, that is. No, I would need paint too. There was so much color in it. Then there is the problem of making you feel the wind. And the smell on the wind.*

Allan was a very tall, powerfully built man with the features of the people of the Pedro Plains that come from the German and French settlers, the Maroons and the good God in heaven knows what other races all blended then burned and etched by the diamond-sharp tropical sun. Leaving, Sonia glanced one last time in the mirror. He stood with his right arm over the woman's shoulder, both smiling now, and a brown dog with a black-tipped, waving tail looking up at them proprietarily. The trees behind them were waving too. Good-bye.

*Nothing in this world could get them down, especially her. They might not have a lot but they are so incredibly lucky. I hope they know it. They look like they ought to live in this paradise forever. Perhaps, just maybe, we could too.*

The American Airlines afternoon flight flew west out of Kingston, paralleling the south coast of the island. Fifteen minutes out of Kingston they had not yet received final clearance to climb to their cruising altitude from the Montego Bay tower, so details of the villages below were still quite clear.

"Look," Sonia said, "Maybe that's your friend still at the office." From the window seat she could see a canoe approaching a much larger boat. The bow cap was bright yellow. To the north she could still see the high ridge of the bluff with the big lighthouse. The sea was unbelievably calm.

"I'm sure it's right where we were. See that Lovers Leap place? And that one fairly decent-looking house just behind the little hill that shelters it. The one they said belongs to the old man they call Mr. James. That's our beach. And I bet that's your happy worker out there going to say hello to some comrade of his. Maybe they're going to share a smoke of ganja or something before they head off home to the wife who will be all dressed up in her head scarf just to greet him." The two boats were still a few yards apart when the body of the aircraft obscured any further view of them.

"Well," she said, "Bye-bye fisherman. Don't forget how lucky you are."

Robert did not say anything about this. He had his

laptop computer on the meal tray and was thinking about real difficulties. All this fairy tale stuff coupled with no-problem types who only had the odd insect to contend with belonged in the past now.

"I wish I had a box of black widow spiders in my luggage," he said, thinking about his bureaucratic foes, "I know where I would put them."

# THE VILLAGE CURTAIN

# THE END OF THE DAY

There was about a half an hour of daylight left when Myra sat down on the very edge of the bluff. The cliff face fell vertical and sheer for three hundred feet straight down to where the low swell probed against the uneven base. The clearly defined edge marking the hundred fathom line running parallel to the shore looked only a few yards out at this place and, for as far as you could see in three directions, the blue face of the sea spread out calm and at rest until it became confused with the horizon. *Pretty weather,* she thought instinctively, in the language of her town. She put her right hand over her dog's shoulders and started to think about what was really going to happen now.

*This is the evening of the fourth day so, you know what that means. It mean that's that. Him not the first and him certainly won't be the last.*

Myra knew it for sure when the last boat got back this morning. That captain knew the boundaries where Allan and his father set every trap and he had the biggest engine in the district so they could cover lots of ground. When they came back she could tell by the look on their faces—you didn't have to ask them anything, except for politeness sake. They said that they had seen the Coast Guard vessel conducting their usual hopeless search and rescue exercise more than fifty miles *up current* from the place where they could have just possibly found the boat with the yellow bow cap that belonged to Allan and his father. Mr. James had called it a "waste of government gas." Mr. James knew a lot of things. Mr. James was a ganja grower.

There was supposed to be an army plane searching as well but no one had seen it. Allan's mother had gone all the way to Kingston to file a report with the

Air Wing. All the formal steps had to be taken or it would have looked very bad on their family. But Myra knew how risky it was. Otherwise, Allan would have never said that by next month he would have his own boat and engine, a seventy-five horsepower at that—no stupid little forty that took five hours to get to the nearest good part of the bank.

*But me did really think it was all right. Really. Allan and his dad had talked to the men outside late at night and me never even looked out to see if me could recognize any of them. So maybe me is all right. Me should a did know it could be like this, but others did it and it had worked out. Me getting old now and not a child of me own and the men laugh and say, "See! Myra's as barren as a mule." And me brother Mickey was in some jail abroad and nobody seemed to know if him would ever get out. So what's the point of being all right? It's not all right. It's all over.*

The Coast Guard people had come to get some more details that morning and everyone was very formal and correct. Among them, Myra had recognized a young officer who had come to the village a year before to explain basic seamanship to men who had fished the Pedro Banks since they were ten years old. They had set up a little stage with safety devices hung behind it and the Member of Parliament had been there. She had felt genuinely sorry for the Member of Parliament because his collar had disappeared completely into the folds of his neck and, although he had three handkerchiefs that looked like small sails, they were not big enough to keep his face dry. The Coast Guard man had told them that an anchor was very important and each boat should have a survival kit.

He asked if anybody had a question and one of the fellows, who liked to put people on the spot, had asked, "How come you no have a flare gun on display?"

The officer put on an official frown and said, "That is still under consideration," as it had been for thirty years, "and your Member of Parliament is on a committee that is working on certain proposals that might

be able to harmonize the firearms act around that issue."
A thicker sweat mask came over the honorable guest's
moon face and a tiny shower fell from his nodding
forehead.

"The gun thing is tricky," the officer said. "We
have a lot of guns on this land. Can't have them at sea too
—so that's a bit troublesome. People can modify flare
guns to fire genuine twelve gauge cartridges." He said
this as if imparting some great, secret gem of wisdom.
There was a fair amount of laughter. Who would bother
fooling around with converting a flare gun into a firearm
when the real thing was so easily attainable?

Myra hoped it had been guns though because, like
lots of fisherman, Allan had a fear of drowning. He must
have seen about a million fish unable to breathe at their
last and maybe it had got inside his brain in some way.
She had told him once that he was awfully close to the
edge of the bluff and he had said, "If you fall off this
place right here you will be dead and dry because of
those flat rocks that stick out at the base. You no have to

drown."

There wasn't a red cent left in their little stash but she had known that. He had said, "The way to really make it is to buy it yourself. When they use their money you're looking at collecting cab fare. And my old man figures that he knows these men. They are going to give him a very special price. Go into Black River and buy two dozen heavy-duty garbage bags and the tape. Buy duct tape. Remember the name. Tell them the tape air-conditioning repairmen use to seal leaks. No buy nothing near here where everybody knows you."

Allan was a thinker, for sure.

"Don't worry," she said. "Everything going to be all right. Me believe in it." She nearly said, *Me believe in you,* but when she said it the other way it sounded more businesslike.

But anyone can make a mistake. When she was a young girl she had seen him make one. They had been out in little a rowboat diving for conch over the grass beds and, when they were finished, he had decided to show them his trick. He was well known for it. He took his little red pocketknife and cut the outside off an orange in a perfect, unbroken spiral and finished with the peel in one hand and the knife in the other. Very professional. Then, at the same time, both hands perfectly coordinated, he would flick the knife shut and toss the coil of orange peel overboard. But this time something went wrong and he snapped the fruit skin down on itself and the knife went sailing into the water. Everybody but Myra screamed with laughter but she just took one good, careful look at the angle of the little red knife sinking through the crystal water to the bottom and went straight after it. She was the best diver of them all anyway and the boat had drifted out from over the conch flats into much deeper water. When she got back to the side of the rowboat her eyes and ears hurt. The knife story was quite famous for a while, although she would invariably have to remind everyone who had got it back. Allan knew she had done it to spare him the embarrassment of having to pretend that the damn knife could stay there. He could no more have dived that deep than walked on the water that covered his prized possession.

*You couldn't do that today old girl. You would have to tie two concrete blocks to yourself to sink with the fat that you have on you. No drowning for you. You would have to float to death.*

The light was going fast now and in another five minutes she wouldn't be able to see the exact features of the cliff base. There was just enough light left to make out the long, flat projections down there. They only stuck out in that one particular place.

Myra stood up.

The dog followed custom. It was the end of the day and he was ready to go home. He was a weather-beaten dog with arthritis and was thinking of the mat in the little house—his comfortable bed. He looked up at Myra, the love of his rough old life, and his eyes filled with fear as the fur on the back of his neck stood up. He was a one-woman dog who had been with her from the days when he was very young, and he knew that his world would never be the same again.

As the sky grew dark, he walked home alone.

# THE VILLAGE CURTAIN

# PART 2

# THE VILLAGE CURTAIN

# MIAMI TIME

Michael, who was serving time for being caught with illegal drugs in South Florida's Biscayne Bay, was acquiring a new skill. He was learning how to tell the precise passage of time by the shifts in the background noises inside the Miami detention center. All his life he had been able to do this by judging the varying shades and angles of daylight, the arrival and departure of the velvet tropical night, and the phases of the moon and the other natural friends that he had been close to. The Miami detention center did not admit these visitors.

On this morning he was also refining another newly discovered ability that was his latest way of getting through the day. He was letting his mind recall everything that he could remember in as much detail as possible and playing it back; seeing how he felt about it and what, if anything, it could teach him. Today he started with the earliest memories of what it was like to pry a tiny living from the waters that washed the beaches of his home village.

In the period of the young moon he would wake instinctively once it had set. This would be the time for him to go. Walking the fifty yards that separated his home from the seashore, he prepared himself for the shock of immersion in the chilly water where he would live until daybreak. No matter how often he did it, there was always that first punch of cold.

There had been fear at first too, but time and confidence had gradually removed it. Now there was just the discomfort, the frustration of finding places where he had previously done well now empty of life, and, sometimes, the excitement of sudden success.

One memorable night he had shot a really big

grouper and it had gone into a cave and lodged itself there. It was not long before daybreak and he had kept vigil over the prize till the light was bright enough to see the apertures and branches in the rock refuge where his opponent sulked. A boat on the way to set traps had come near enough that he got their attention and one of the men aboard had a gaff and lent it to him. He had gaffed the grouper and with the leverage of the gaff handle he could get enough pressure to break the fish free. It was the biggest fish he had ever caught in his night diving career.

Along the parallel reef that fringed the coast where he lived, all the extractive fishing methods had already run their course. The only rocks that he could reach were devoid of everything but the smallest specimens. The glass-bottom boat tour guides operating further west, where the hotels were located, pointed out the brilliant rock formations and tried to be ever-ready with hasty deflections to questions such as this:

"How come there don't seem to be much fish around, man?"

"Sometimes they just go and hide, suh."

But in the quiet hours of the real dark, the last and most cautious of the survivors poked their much-hunted noses carefully out from the deepest recesses of the caves and tangled weed beds and drifted, wraith-like, over the sea floor to feed on whatever had survived the multiple assaults upon their gradually dying world. You can push the creatures of the sea to near extinction, but they were there in the primordial cradle of life before humanity and will certainly be there after their most efficient and deadly enemy is gone.

It was in these midnight hours that Michael mounted patrol and glided among them through the coal-black sea with his two most prized possessions: an underwater flashlight and his homemade spear gun. He too was fighting a survival action and would do so as long as he could.

On a good half night, he would get four or five pounds of fish and occasionally a small lobster or two. He stalked them either side of the moonlight and only abandoned his foraging if the moon was full, or near to it, or the sea turbulent and the visibility poor. When he got home, his mother would give him a cup of steaming mint tea to warm him up. His father, who had been a diver himself before his stroke and was now living on borrowed time, would remind Michael that it would be a good idea to try and sleep for an hour or two before he set off for school.

At eight, which would have been the latest that he should leave, his mother often tried to wake him—but not too hard—and left him, as she had done many times before, thinking *there is only so much he can do*. She would not have had to wake his sister, Myra, because she would have been up at daybreak and gone down to the beach to congratulate Michael on whatever he had caught. That was their ritual.

"What you got today, Mickey?" She had been the only person in the world to call him that.

"Six. And a big spider crab and two chicken lobster."

"You is the best fisherman in the world! Me picked mint for you and give it to Ma."

That was the way it had been. He would try and keep this mental film show going as long as possible, thinking of his boyhood friends: Frankie, Louis, Leo, Allan and Eva. In this hard, cold place he thought especially of Eva, who had come one night to where he was sitting on a rock near the little river setting live baited trot lines to catch snook. She had walked up to him purposefully and said, "Me just come back from the tent." She was holding her shoes in one hand. Eva was about fourteen years old. Michael was two years older, but only in time.

The tent was a visiting revivalist preacher's portable crusade and had been in operation at the village every night for a week. It would be moving down the coast once the organizers had collected all they could squeeze from the congregation. The chief speaker was a white evangelical fundamentalist from the United States and he had a sound system that you could hear all the way from the next town. The music was loud even down by the river. It was a powerful, rhythmic hymn about what happened to sinners. Fire and drums. Even this far away, you could make out some of the words: *Fire, fire, think about the fire!* Bang, bang went the bass drum.

"You learn about God?" Michael asked her.

"Don't joke about that. We can talk about God later. Me no listen to the man. Me listen to the music. Come down here on the sand, feel how it warm! Make me show you what the music can do." She dropped the shoes and held out her hand to him. That was Eva.

But presently his problem was getting through the morning inside the Miami detention center. Sinners were everywhere around him in here. Honest to God sinners.

Michael's nose still hurt from the recent incident when a Cuban gangster had gone after a little scrawny inmate known as Mouse. Michael had been in the way when the Cuban swung at Mouse with a piece of chain. The flying end had broken Michael's nose in error. The Cuban had said, "Sorry man, I'll get that mangy skeleton good next time. I'll give him an extra one for you." But Mouse was under a general protective watch ever since and had suddenly obtained some sort of trusty status so, for the moment, he was okay. Now the Cuban had a new, updated chain that was shorter and, according to him, much more accurate. Thus Mouse faced an uncertain future.

Michael went back to his pastime. He could make the pictures but there was still a lot missing. He was suffering from one of the major handicaps that recollections entail; it is impossible to precisely reconstruct scent by purely mental effort when you are awake. If you are asleep or, even half asleep, it can happen. At least that's the way it seems. Michael shut his eyes.

"Wake up Jammy," a warder said, running a baton along the cell window. "You going to see the boss." Every Jamaican in the prison was called Jammy. There were quite a few.

In the warden's office Michael got the news. He

was going to get an early release because the prison was severely overcrowded. That was what they were doing to keep in line with a government formula dealing with inmate capacity. He would be deported and barred from reentry to the land of the free and the home of the brave.

"But you are specially favored, Jammy," the warden observed. "There's plenty in here longer than you that didn't get picked. You know any of the right people?"

"If me did know the right people me would never be in here."

"I guess not, if I knew the right people I wouldn't be here myself."


Mouse came to Michael's door about midday. He looked as gaunt and flaky as ever. If you were going to make a drawing of what a social reject and typical convict ought to look like you would probably come up with a portrait of Mouse. He certainly suited the part. "I heard about it," he said. "You're a good guy. Maybe I'll see you again some day."

"Not in here." Michael told him. "You going to have to come and see me at home."

# MR. ANDERSON INTERVENES

When Jimmy arrived to open the bar he saw Mr. Anderson sitting outside in a police car. "Hello Super," Jimmy said, raising the visitor's rank. Jimmy knew Mr. Anderson was an inspector but, as a Kingston-based senior member of a feared island-wide operational squad, he qualified as an honorary superintendent this far out in rural Jamaica.

"Lets go inside, Jimmy," Mr. Anderson said, starting towards the door. "Before anyone else gets here."

The weathered, red sign on the bar read Cool Breeze Spot. It was cool inside and smelled of mildew, but it was a clean bar. That is not so easy to find near a fishing beach where it takes a real effort to discourage flies. If you put up screens then you block the wind and nobody comes in.

"Now look, Jimmy, I'm just here to tidy up a file. I'm not here to put anyone in any special trouble. But, do me a favor, and don't bother lying to me. It insults my intelligence." Anderson was a film buff. He wore a raincoat like Colombo in ninety degree weather and he liked that line about insulting his intelligence; he tried to make it sound as cool as Al Pacino did when he was Michael Corleone in *The Godfather*. The contradiction in characters didn't bother the inspector. Roles in his world were always blurred anyway.

"Super, go ahead. But me hear lots of stuff in here that's just rum talk. You don't want to trust it too much."

"Jimmy, since when you got yourself a dog?" Mr. Anderson glanced down at the old brown dog that was laying beneath the bar.

"That dog belonged to a woman who fell or

whatever off the bluff. He started hanging about the place and me let him sleep here now. But him have a problem, Super. He's turning into an alcoholic. A rum head. The boys pour white rum in his bowl. It started as a joke, you know. Someone said, 'Here, have a drink and cheer up,' cause he looks kind of downhearted all the time and it got to be a habit with them and him too. Most nights after seven him can't walk straight."

"I knew a goat like that out in St. Thomas at a bar in Yallahs. Used to stand outside waiting for the place to open and leave when he had enough. Got run over crossing the road one night. Must have been blind drunk. For years after he died people would say 'Meet you in the goat bar.' "

"That's a great story Super." Jimmy didn't think it was any better than his own dog story, particularly with the star present, but he was being carefully courteous as usual.

"Anyway, what I want to know, Jimmy, is this. Those fellows who went missing—I understand. You don't have to explain that to me. But I want to close this file and the part I want to know for certain is about the woman. This same woman who owned this rum drinking dog. Is she a part of it? I mean, you said it yourself. She fell or whatever. So tell me straight. Did she get murdered? Because if that was part of it I'm going to put the whole thing on a different level. If they kill each other at sea in some stupid drug fight frankly it's not going to keep me awake but if someone comes right inside here and rubs this woman out it's a different thing. You must see that?"

"Super, you tell me not to lie to you and I respect that. But the whole thing is nobody really knows about that scene exactly. I mean—she must have been upset. Maybe she just got desperate. She only had her brother Michael left and him was in prison in Florida lockup at the time. None of us did know he was close to being deported. You know him just got back about a week after the whole thing?"

"Of course I know that. But he was locked up in

Miami on drug charges you know. Do you think there was some connection?"

"Super, these people find each other one way or another. Maybe. Maybe not."

"Look at this." Mr. Anderson put a half a sheet of paper on the bar; it had two lines of writing on it. "You see that? That's the name of a boat. And the two dates are inward clearance dates at the port of Black River. That first date is the first time she came in. See the second one?"

Jimmy could read it without moving. The second inward clearance date was today.

"They say they are here to buy kingfish. Maybe. Maybe not. The nets are already killing that out but I suppose you can still get a small cargo. You think you can find out anything about it for me?"

"I'll ask my father, Super. As you wish." Jimmy was a bit more formal now that he had been officially recruited.

"You do that, son. I really just want to close the

file but I have to go through the motions. I just came down here to get up-to-date information. Ask your dad. He always seems to know a lot of things."

Watching the car drive away, Jimmy thought it was interesting that Mr. Anderson had actually given *him* information. Surely he could have closed his file with what he had and not bothered to drive all the way down here. Was he just demonstrating to his boss in Kingston that he had paid a formal visit to the area before he signed off on the case? Maybe he just turned into a total bureaucrat, him and his file. Thinking about it, Jimmy knew better.

The two men walked over to where the trawler *Salvation* was loading fish at Hendricks Dock in the port. The captain was sitting on the transom watching while his two man crew weighed the baskets. It was a sparkling morning.

"Hello, Frankie," the captain said. "You got any fish to bring over?"

"Not right now, Cap, but is okay we come aboard for a minute?" The three of them went into the forward cabin. The captain sat in the helmsman's chair and the two visitors stood.

"Cap," Frankie said, "this is Mikey. Me have a little problem. Me can't come up with all the cash it's going to take. Me want to bring him into it with me. Me know him a long time. Me guarantee him completely. Everything will be just like how we did agree but him wants to come with me just to see that his money's safe. You can understand that?"

The captain turned to Michael. "What happened to your face?"

"Captain, I got a little difficulty with balance. Me fall down sometimes. Me broke my nose a few times."

"You ever fall out of a boat?"

"Not yet, but me sit as much as me can."

"Strictly the two of you, understand?" The captain spoke directly to Frankie, but he included Michael in what he was saying. "Don't come back here under any circumstances. I will call you tomorrow night and give you the GPS coordinates where you are to go. You understand I am a serious man. Don't mess around with any of that 'soon come' island foolishness. I can make a deal with lots of people and I know lots of people. Big people. Big people in the police force. I make it my business to know all the right people. You understand?"

"That's cool, Cap." Frankie looked uncomfortable. After all, he was a captain in his own right and he owned his own boat. He really did not like people speaking to him like this but there was a lot at stake, so he took it.

The swell was from the southeast, as usual, but there was hardly any wind. The canoe rolled broadside, waiting as the day came on. They had been there for three hours and by the time *Salvation* showed on the horizon it was bright, hot, and clear.

Frankie started the old forty-horsepower and came up slowly on the starboard side of the trawler. They put two lines, bow and stern, on her to secure the two boats parallel alongside but the swell made it troublesome so the captain dropped two fenders between the two vessels then pulled them tight together. Michael stood up and lifted one of the heavy bales.

"Hold on, boy," the captain said. "Pick one of your square groupers out of the middle and give it to me. I want to have a look at what I'm buying."

Grouper is the one of the most valuable fish and the nickname "square grouper" had become common for the rectangular shaped parcels in which marijuana was commonly packed. Michael pulled one of the plastic wrapped, well-taped packages from the center of the pile and put it on the rail of the trawler. The everlasting swell heaved and he looked like he could hardly keep his stance. The packet fell off the rail and slid across the afterdeck. The two crewmen stopped it at the far side of the transom and one opened a clasp knife. The captain momentarily looked astern to see that they were ready to cut it open.

Frankie reached under the old sack that made a

kind of cushion on the thwart of the canoe and pulled out a shotgun. Michael had the nine-millimeter out by then and only one man immediately realized what was coming. Although the shotgun blast took off the captain's right arm and a fair amount of chest with it, Michael only hit the man with the knife.

The other crewman made for the cabin across the rolling deck and fell as he made it to the door of the wheelhouse. Frankie got aboard and put two more shells into the shotgun. He saw the man trying to get something from under the navigation table and threw the shotgun to Michael who was now aboard and near the cabin door. On a rolling platform marksmanship is uncertain but the two barrels of a shotgun at close range make that irrelevant.

The captain and the knife man were still alive after that so Michael shot them cleanly through the head with the handgun. The whole thing had taken about a minute. Maybe two.

They tied the three bodies together then bound the

soggy group to the steel capstan. Frankie opened the engine room hatch and broke off the main water inlet fitting that fed the engine's cooling pump. Then he went forward and did the same with all the below-the-waterline valves that he could find. By the time he came back on deck the engine compartment was halfway flooded. The whole afterdeck was awash. Michael was cutting the taped packages open and scattering the leaves and other trash that they contained into the ocean. A long green trail began to form like a weed line.

They waited until *Salvation* slipped down by the stern. The ancient, secret keeping sea closed over her. Running home with the swell behind them the old forty made reasonable time.

"What you going to go do now Mikey?" Frankie asked. "You going back into this fishing business?"

"No way boy, me going to work for Jimmy's father on the farm up in the hills. Maybe at the Co-Op in the ice house where the fish is kept, if him want. Me never did love this sea-thing plenty. Me had enough of it when me was a boy. It's all right, you know—if you can go out when you feel like it. If you can't do that it's punishment. Pure punishment. And me going to take my sister's dog up into the mountains with me. Me no like seeing him turning into a barfly. Him got a few good years left in him—him not a bad old dog."

Remembering those merciful single-spaced head shots Frankie said, "Mikey, you know what? You really is nothing but a soft-hearted son-of-a-bitch."

# THE WORLD COMES TO VISIT

Driving up an unpaved road that led to nowhere in particular, the dubious legacy of a forgotten politician in the Parish Council who had got hold of a bit of money at some time in the past, Mr. James hoped that the morning rain would soon work its way further inland. There were no windscreen wipers on his old Land Rover. Though he knew the road perfectly, sections of it kept falling into the bordering valley so it would have been reassuring to be able to see properly.

By the time he got to where the funds and the road had stopped, the screen of rain had been blown north over the high mountains. In ten minutes, the sun would be back and the steaming smell of the dripping rainforest would be all around him. It was about a half mile walk from here to the little clearing where the tiny farm house stood.

When he was thirty feet from the building, the old dog announced his arrival with a single bark of approval. A stranger would have gotten an earful. This was just a doorbell type of bark to advise the people inside.

"Hello, Mikey," Mr. James said, "How's it going?"

"Fine, Chief. You saw the rain?"

"Just enough. That's just what it needs at this time." Mr. James sat down on the miniature porch, which was really just an overhang of the main roof with a rough wooden deck beneath and three plastic chairs. Eva came out.

"You want anything, suh?" she asked, smiling at Mr. James. She would have had the most perfect set of white teeth except two of the front ones were missing. Local dentistry was aware of only one treatment for all problems.

"You got any coconut water? I drink it for my blood pressure."

Eva slipped on her shoes and went to fetch a coconut from the stream that ran at the back of the house. She always tried to keep a few submerged in the spring where they kept as cool as in any refrigerator. In her absence, Mr. James explained to Michael that he wanted him to come down to the village. He told Michael that he wanted him to look at someone who said that he had known Michael during his time in Florida. A white man with a little straggly beard. Looked like a hippie sort. Looked like a druggie, actually.

It was easier now going down the hill with the rain over. Mr. James stopped before he got to the bend in the main road. Once you came around that you could see the village but, of course, anyone there could see you too.

"Now I'm going to drop you off here and you walk the rest of the way by yourself. Go down and walk along the beach. I'll wait here for you and take you back.

I'm not even going to go down by the seaside. Take your time, Mikey." Mr. James settled back in the driver's seat. "I can't keep my eyes open."

Entering the bar Michael wasn't sure if he should make the first move but the newcomer solved that by putting a scrawny arm over his shoulder and greeting him by name.

"What brings you here, Mouse?" Michael asked him.

"Looking for you, man."

"How did you know where me was?"

"After you got shipped out I found out from one of the other boys where you came from. I mean really came from, not just the island. Hell, I knew that from your accent, Jammy. I wanna talk to you, man. Can we take a walk somewhere?"

Outside, the sea breeze had signed on for the day bringing the salty, open-ocean smell across the broad expanse of the beach. A boat was being unloaded at the waterside and everyone was crowding around observing the catch: criticizing, commenting, and weighing portions of it. Michael and Mouse stopped at where an almond tree grew right out of the sand. It was an old tree and a hurricane that had passed just south of the island had lopped off all the higher branches. The tree now seemed unwilling to reach upwards into the dangerous, unpredictable upper air and had grown out horizontally producing an almost black patch of shade. There was an overturned boat in this place. The owner had made a few sporadic attempts to render it seaworthy but had apparently become appalled at what he was encountering as the work progressed and had hopefully painted "For Sale" along both sides. At some later date, finally facing reality, he had added in another color, "CHEAP." The two men sat, where many had before, on the flat bottom of this testimony to failed maritime investment.

"You look okay Mike", Mouse said. "You put on a bit of weight."

"You look the same. How long since you got out?"

"Just a while. They got this system where they can only have a certain amount of inmates no matter what. A capacity ceiling, they call it. So when they get new ones they have to parole older ones. In a facility like that it's just a matter of time. That's what happened to you, right? Plus it's mixed up, you know. Nobody seems to know what the hell the policy is. You can just get called anytime and you're back on the street."

Mouse raised his head and looked directly at Michael. "Now I want to say something to you straight off. That time I just couldn't do anything for you, man. The staff there never did cut me any slack and if I had tried to do anything, intervene or anything like that, they'd have stuck me in the hole. I'm sorry about your nose and all that, but it don't look that bad. I mean, it's just a nose."

"That's all right, Mouse. It's just a nose. You're right. It still can work."

"But look, Mike, that bartender guy—Jimmy—he said you're trying to get back into the fishing business. He said you're just crewing on different boats. You ain't going to get nowhere doing that, right? I got a plan and I got some big backers. But I got to find a solid local connection to make a buy. Can you help me with that?"

"Mouse," Michael sounded resigned. "You came to the wrong man and the wrong place. Me know me got mixed up in that scene in America but me was up there with no papers anyway. Here me get by. It's tough; and me no like being just a sometimes extra hand hanging around the beach all day. But me put up with it. The thing is, you can't pull anything that even *looks* funny anywhere round here. They got undercover police. Army snoops. Local informers. They all over the place like cockroaches. Even in the hills you can't grow one little patch of stuff or they'll have some plane that can find it. If someone gets lost at sea they can't never have an aircraft available to search for it but, plant a little weed under a banana tree and the next thing happens is there's a helicopter landing on the nearest road with a whole bunch of cops with dogs. Anyway that's what the farmers tell me. Forget it, man. Anyhow forget it *here*. A few miles up the coast it might be different. Other places got protection, maybe. Maybe them know the right people. But this spot is out of the question. Fool with that and everyone on the outside will hear in a day or two. Even that guy, Jimmy. You can't trust him."

Mouse looked thoughtful and sad but he wasn't quite finished. "Can you give me even a name up the line then? Maybe just an introduction? I got to take something back with me or my people are going to quit on me. They bought the ticket, man."

"Forget it, Mouse. Better you don't even bring that kind of thing up. It might put you in some trouble just talking about it."

"Well, thanks Mike. I see what you mean. Good luck with the fishing."

"It getting harder all the time." Everybody agreed on that.

Mr. James was dozing in his seat in the Land Rover. He

had let his old farmer-style straw hat slip forward just a little as his concession to sleep. He looked like the portrait of a patient grandfather to whom you would go for a lesson in old-world values. He woke up as Michael reached the passenger door.

"What's it look like, Mikey?"

"There's something wrong with it, Chief. When them held me in Miami them took my passport away and me never got it back. When me was being deported me heard it was mislaid. Me didn't even give the court in Miami the right name of the town where me come from and me definitely never told nobody in the lock-up. Me know better than that. So him full of shit when him say that he got that from somebody on the inside. That much me can tell you for true."

"Well. It's all right Mikey. That's quite all right."

Mr. James remembered his coconut water back at the farmhouse. Eva had cut the top off and had brought it, ready to drink, right from the nut in the traditional way, but they had left already so she had poured it into a glass bottle and put it in the stream. By now it would be as cold as the spring itself. Eva went and got it. While they had been gone she had tied her brightly colored headscarf over her hair so as to be ready for their return. That was Eva.

It was so intensely hot in the Criminal Investigation Branch's office on East Queen Street that Mr. Anderson had reluctantly hung his raincoat over a nail in the wall. The woman constable, who was his assistant in every way, brought the visitor in and went out shutting the door behind her thereby bringing the temperature inside the cramped room up by a few degrees.

"Mr. Elliot," Mr. Anderson said, "You are so kind to come in to see me. With the level of connection your agency has out here sometimes we only hear about you fellows after you have left. You couldn't have been here too long or the Jamaican jerk pork and patties and Red Stripe beer would have put a few pounds on you. You're lucky to be so thin, though. Better in the heat, eh? I hope you had a productive visit?"

"Well, Inspector, you always learn something but, I must say, you guys seem to be getting a real handle on most of the places along the coast. It's impressive. I know it's not easy. It's nice to see so many people turning to honest, decent work. Like this kingfish netting project. It looks like a wonderful venture. Just what the country needed. I hear they have two boats working at it now. One on each end of the island."

Mr. Anderson did not comment on this.

"So, Sir, I want to say again that I plan to give you all very high marks. I am certain that my report will be excellent grounds for future funding in our cooperative efforts. I will take the report to Carlos myself when I get back to Miami. By the way, do you know anything about *Salvation*?"

Anderson looked sharply at the gaunt figure before him. He put on the expression of a man trying to understand a remark so incomprehensible as to be almost lunatic. "I'm not a religious man."

"Oh, not that kind of salvation, Inspector. I'm talking about a boat called *Salvation*. A converted trawler. She made two trips to Black River to buy kingfish from that very project I just mentioned. But on her way back from the second voyage she simply disappeared. Vanished. Not even a distress call. Not a sighting. Nothing. And she had a satellite phone on board. I know it can happen but it would have to be something awful fast."

"Well, it does happen, Mr. Elliot. Every now and then we lose a boat somewhere around the island without a trace. Maybe some ship runs them down. There's all kinds of weird shipping tramping around the oceans these days."

Mr. Elliot looked like he would have liked to say something but Mr. Anderson was giving him no opening.

"Do you know what happened when the Soviet Union broke up? There were hundreds of Russian ships in ports all over the world. Suddenly the state goes bust and you know what the crews did? They stole them.

Honest to God. They changed the names, chopped the identification numbers off the engines, and registered them in Panama or Liberia or wherever and started their own freight line with their new asset. They did pretty well too because they took any cargo from wherever they were to anywhere they were asked to go at prices no normal freighter could compete against. I mean, after all, they got the ship free. They're all over the place still. Especially South America and Africa. I guess parts of Asia too. All over."

"That's interesting, Inspector." He rubbed his chin where he had shaved off his beard earlier that morning. "I never knew that. But, look here—I promised I would ask about this boat *Salvation*."

Mr. Anderson stood up; the heat in the office was unbearable and he was feeling thirsty.

Mr. Elliot continued, "You see the captain of it was a close personal friend of the head of my division. Carlos himself. They were in the army together and this captain guy had a run of hard luck so my boss helped stake him with some agency funding so he could go into the fish carrying business. The captain was going to keep his eyes open for us at the same time, you know. My chief said that he thought the captain was on to something but that it might take a while to build up confidence and then, just like that, the whole boat goes and vanishes. It makes you wonder. And, look here, Inspector, you know my boss. He ain't never going to let something like that just slide. He's like a vindictive elephant when it comes to something like that. You know what he's like."

"I'll certainly make inquiries and let you know if anything crops up, Mr. Elliot."  Mr. Anderson considered this new animal description for Carlos, who was a highly placed operative in the D.E.A. in Miami and perhaps other agencies. Anderson had always thought of him as a spider but Mr. Elliot ought to know more about him so he would keep that in mind. He looked meaningfully towards the door, eager to end the conversation and get some fresh air.

Mr. Elliot appeared as though he would have

dearly loved to hang around and explore the *Salvation* issue but, with Mr. Anderson clearly impatient, he seemed a little unsure how to manage that. The effort of serving up the missing boat and crew as seamlessly as he had done seemed to have drained him a little. He had had a hard time dealing with the return Mr. Anderson had fired at him with all that about the unorthodox reform of the Russian Merchant Marine. Could that be true? Could crime on such a scale go unpunished?

"Are we sending him to the airport, Arlene?" Mr. Anderson asked the woman constable when Mr. Elliot had eventually left the stifling little office.

"In what, Roy?" Arlene asked, "You think we have any cars to spare driving foreign skeletons around? You want me to send yours?"

"Good God, no. Never mind. Forget it. Let's go down the road and have a cold drink."

He took his raincoat off the wall. He could at least carry it with him. He had been in the police racket for over twenty years and was considering his approaching retirement, although he just couldn't leave. There was the pension to consider. When he was a little boy the village policeman had been a super-sized figure to him and, one day, he had been with his father and the old man had stopped to speak to this uniformed giant.

"Hello Roy," the policeman had said.

"Hello Officer, can I ask you something?"

"Sure."

"What made you become a policeman?"

He still remembered the answer. "I became a policeman so I could protect all of you in the village." He had felt quite safe for a long time after that.

# THE MEN WITH THE NET

A beach seine net must be one of the most ancient forms of fishing. Certainly it has a medieval look about it with the power being entirely supplied by the muscles, endurance, and skill of the men who haul it ashore. In some countries they tie donkeys to rotating, capstan-type devices and lead them around in everlasting circles to apply pressure to the ropes that bring this type of net onto the beach but that system has never been used in Jamaica. Jamaican donkeys are among the most stubborn members of that notoriously independent breed and might express their boredom and hostility at this use of their talents by faking dizziness and falling down, rolling their eyes, and generally behaving as though they couldn't survive after a few circuits.

The strongest and most patient men of the village are recruited to draw on the two ends of the great arc of rope and mesh for the four or five hours that it takes to bring an average size beach seine to where the bag, or final constricted purse, is brought up and out of the water.

The normal method of laying out this device is for one end of the net to be pulled out into the bay by boat and set in as large a half moon shape as the length of the contraption will allow, with the top rope floated by hundreds of corks, while the foot rope has lead weights spaced at roughly the same intervals as the corks above them. This creates a massive fence with either end having very long (and strong) ropes that are led back to the shore. A gang of anywhere from six to ten men begin to pull steadily on these ropes and, little by little, the seine begins to close as it sweeps slowly inland enveloping everything in its path.

Unfortunately, the sea floor is never free from obstacles like rocks, coral heads, and sunken logs, so the boat's work shifts from the setting phase to the keeping-clear phase where one or two divers watch the curvature of the float line to see if it begins to lose its perfect arc. If it starts to develop a slight "V" this indicates that the weighted line is hitched on some immovable feature on the seafloor and the diver must investigate and clear the blockage so that things may proceed smoothly. Please bear in mind that the normal hours for this type of fish entrapment in most places are between midnight and daybreak, when it is easier to sneak up on species that have moved close to the beach and out of their daylight haunts among the fringing reef.

This diving business has its challenges. In pitch-black water, this diver (or divers) must disentangle the mesh and lead-weighted foot rope from a variety of snags. If you have ever tried to pick a veil from a cactus in bright daylight on land you may contemplate the problem of clearing transparent nylon netting, ten feet underwater, from jagged stones in the middle of the night. This cannot be done in too leisurely a manner for the fish are getting suspicious and starting to notice that they keep bumping into a fence that never used to be there and wondering exactly what in hell should be done about it. Only their natural instinct works in the fishermen's favor; to head outwards toward their regular refuge in the reef. If they all made one concentrated rush to the very shallowest part where the ocean meets the sand, they might find that the ends of the net have not yet closed the corral. If that gate is still open and consists only of the strand of rope that is tightening the trap, the result of half a night's toil would be zero.

The diving team and the man servicing their boat platform receive lots of shouted encouragement to make it snappy from the beach parties in language that is as forceful as the pullers can devise. "If you don't get that free don't bother come back ashore. Drown yourself!" would be an exceptionally mild warning while descriptions of the diver's family history and unusual sexual preferences are voiced in megaphone proportions by fellows with very fine lungs indeed.

In between these exchanges, because the boys in the boat have a few comments to make on the ancestry and masculinity of the gangs hauling away too, the director of this whole production—usually the owner of the net—calls intermittently to the group at one end or the other: "Walk down!" or "Walk up!" Down is west and up is east, since the prevailing sea wind is from the east about three hundred days out of the year, and up is up-wind while down is down-wind. These up and down commands are designed to create an equal encirclement with the whole seine so the reinforced center, the purse, will be the last part to come ashore. This two thousand yard dance and massive expenditure of energy is timed to conclude as near as possible to dawn so that they will get to see, in the coming of the light, what is actually inside the bulging, flapping, slashing mass of desperate, captured marine life that have now discovered what is really happening and are disputing the outcome to the absolute best of their ability.

Everything alive, along with a lot of inanimate objects, is all bundled up together in this angry purse. Snook, snapper, rocks, seaweed, rays, porcupine fish, nurse sharks, herring, mullet, shad, a dead cat, a few fence posts, sea eggs, ribbon fish and lots of other interesting usable and useless contents are spilling out among peoples' legs and keeping boredom away.

A word on these ribbon fish mentioned just now. They are more commonly called cutlass fish in the Caribbean. It is a more fitting name than the rather innocent sounding word *ribbons* by which they are known along the east coast of America. Brilliant silver, like a polished machete, they have a mouth crowded with barbed teeth. As the seine net makes its final landing these shining, lance-like fish, built like flattened eels, launch their bodies skyward and dozens of them make it well clear of the top rope. During this last stage of bringing the catch to shore a few men will be detailed to hold this rope as high as possible to keep the more prized, but less acrobatic, mullet from leaping out. If trusted with this task, it is imperative to keep a sharp eye out for the cutlass fish in flight. His habit of jumping with his mouth wide open will mean that if a sharp eye is not kept well trained it will cease to be a functioning eye at all. Let that happen to you twice (once in each orb) and you will not be allowed to participate in this fun anymore.

"Walk down, walk down!" Mr. James called out, seated on the bumper of his venerable Land Rover parked back on the hard sand.

Easing on the strain as he took twenty paces west, Frankie noticed a slight form almost concealed behind the line of sea grape trees which grew where the sand became mixed with earth about twenty feet back from the sea front. The waning moon had begun her climb some two hours ago and pale light fingered its way between the dense foliage so he could just make out the darkness shift when the figure moved. Anyone local would be unlikely to stay back there but he was busy and tucked his observation away. He concentrated more on looking for an unusual swirl or wake on the shining water in case it proved to be a menace of some kind, such as a big shark prowling the perimeter of the net.

Every time he walked west, closing the distance between himself and the other gang, he would scan the tree line. Since seeing something quickly was essential in his trade, he would catch the fleeting irregularity in the well known, moonlight sprinkled landscape each time it moved.

"Go on in and hold up, Frankie," Mr. James ordered him as the first, finer mesh of the purse came ashore. Frankie dropped the head line and waded into the water where the cutlass fish had already started to make their aerial exits. He was now facing the beach instead of looking out to sea and had even less opportunity to take discerning looks at the mysterious figure in the background now that the shining half circles of teeth were flying past him. The overlapping crown of the swollen purse closed over the bulging mass and finally cut off all the overhead access to freedom as the catch was pulled completely clear of the water and up onto the apron of sand.

The sky was fairly bright with the coming of the day but Mr. James started the engine of his Land Rover, enabling him to turn on the headlights, and positioned the old vehicle so that the contents of the bag became easier to see. The boat came ashore and was hauled up. The divers got out and traded a few final insults with the beach crew.

"You pull like old woman."

"The old drunken dog with arthritis that Mikey have can dive better than you."

And so on.

Frankie walked directly up to the shelter where the little form stood. It was a young white woman in a nightgown. If he had found a mermaid in the now being emptied net it wouldn't have been more shocking.

"Jesus, lady, what happened to you?" Frankie was looking at her properly now. Her face looked like it had been run over by Mr. James's Land Rover. She was white all right, but her face was all colors.

She mumbled something to him and Frankie asked, "You want to hide your face?" That's what he thought she had asked for.

This time she tried harder to speak through the damage. "I need a place to hide."

He got it that time. "Hold on, just you hold on."

They were sitting in the Co-Op building where the fish were being weighed out. Some vendors had already got all they could manage to sell. Michael was packing ice in layers over the ones that would be going across the island to the north coast for the hotels that had standing orders with them. Frankie had taken the beat-up woman to his little house on the very outskirts of the village and his wife had given her a series of rags chilled by soaking in ice water to wrap around her head and cheeks. After he heard the woman's story, Frankie had come over to the Co-Op and explained the thing as best he could to Mr. James sitting at the table by the big scale. As far as he could understand, she had walked the three and a half miles from the hotel that stood about mid-distance between their village and the next.

Her boyfriend had done all that damage to her earlier in the night and, when he had gone to sleep, she had taken all the money from his wallet and climbed over the hotel wall so that the security guards at the front gate would have no trace of her leaving. She had walked along the beach without knowing where she was going till she saw the lights and people on the sand and stood watching, trying to figure out what to do next. All she knew was that each time it was worse than the last and maybe he would kill her soon.

"I just want to hide," she said. She had said it a lot of times.

Mr. James looked at Frankie. He liked Frankie very much. He might very well be related to him in some way. So he wanted Frankie to understand what had to be done, without disrespecting him in any way, because he knew that the younger men put a lot of emphasis on respect. He did too, in his own old-fashioned way. "What exactly you want me to do, Frankie?"

Frankie had thought about that too. He thought about the little farmhouse in the clearing with the healing, scented forest all around and the cold mountain spring running just past the back door. He thought about the old, friendly dog that soaked up affection as he soaked up the sun, laying out in the clearing with the heat seeping into his creaky bones. It would take about a half a day to knock up a one room extension to the place. Nobody outside really knew the place existed. He thought of Eva, who lived there with Michael and was a highly capable and tender hearted soul with a wonderful ability to understand and appreciate things without saying much. He put all that to Mr. James, sitting there in the fishy-smelling distribution room at the Co-Op.

"She could stay there for a while, boss. We could put her on the next boat going up with some stuff. She got some money. Hell, she's an American. They could put her ashore anywhere on the coast up there and she could disappear."

"Look here, Mikey." Mr. James called out.

Michael came out of the cold room. Mr. James explained Frankie's plan carefully to him. He was still maintaining the properly constructed atmosphere of an elder, canvassing wisdom, but reasonably sure of the verdict. That's why he had given Michael the responsibility of overseeing the farm in the first place. Frankie looked at Michael. "It'll be okay Mikey. I know it going to be. You got a soft heart. I know you got a soft heart." He was remembering how it had been.

Michael looked straight at Frankie. Nothing had changed between them so he spoke honestly to the boy who had grown up with him. "But not a soft head, Frankie. Me no have a soft head." He went back to where the ice was packed in big blocks waiting to be broken up into usable portions.

"Frankie," said Mr. James, "listen to me. Go over to Jimmy and tell him to give you a bottle of white rum. Tell him to *give* it to you. Tell him I said to do that. I'll go over to your house and pick the lady up. By the time you get there she'll be gone. Go to bed. You worked all night and you're dead beat. You're tired and jumpy. Get some sleep. I'm going to take her into the Black River police station. I'll get Roy Anderson to call the sergeant. They'll put the fear of God into the boyfriend when he gets there. If that works then so be it. But this is an outside thing. Other things, maybe not. But this is not our business. It's an outside matter. I love you, Frankie. But you have to understand these things."

# THE BIG FISH

The use of mesh wire fish traps makes up at least fifty percent of the commercial fishery in Jamaica. Maybe they account for more—nobody really knows. There are a lot of environmentalists who object to these pots. Hundreds go missing every year from weather related reasons and others from having the marking buoys cut off by passing vessels. These pots become unattended killing machines for some time after that happens. Fishermen claim that this is not really as damaging as it sounds. They say that entrapped fish die from the abrasions caused by endless circling within the steel mesh if a pot is not hauled and emptied regularly. When this begins to happen sharks, rays, big eels, and other powerful scavengers tear the lost pot to pieces to get at the spoiling carcasses within. There is obviously some truth to this.

Certainly the traps are far less deadly than the nylon (or plastic) reef nets, which are set as close as possible to the rocky outcrops where the fish congregate. These nets get hitched in the craggy bottom and are frequently torn free when being taken up, leaving sections of this almost indestructible material draped between the coral heads. Eventually, crabs cut this fence of death as they use their claws to extract whatever snags its gills in the still intact webbing but, as long as any functioning sections remain, more victims will get entangled.

Most of the wire traps, set in anywhere from forty to one hundred fifty feet of water, are drawn aboard the tending vessel by pulling the pot to the surface, having located the point where it was set by a rope connected to one or two floats. The only exceptions to this are the ones that are stolen by prowlers—professional divers, equipped with scuba tanks, who cut the buoyed rope that is supposed to mark the trap's location and then reset them in new places. After a while these divers, who get to know a stretch of sea floor as well as their own backyard, can amass a better collection of fish pots than the people who paid to build them in the first place. The new underwater trap owners, who invariably claim to be righteous spear fisherman, shoot the fish inside with their spear guns otherwise skeptics might question how they have so many fish in their boat without any wounds. Now nobody can say, "How the hell you have all those fish without any holes in them and you say you are a genuine spear fisherman? Something wrong!" In any case, it is the best way to get the prey out of the underwater enclosure since you can't open the trap door through which the fish would be poured out into a boat.

Occasionally when the coast is clear and there are a lot of fish in the trap, the diver will attach a temporary rope to the cage and have his partner in crime pull the trap up and quickly empty it in the approved manner, but they will still have to run a spear through each fish in preparation for the possibility of being questioned. There's always some problem and people, especially people who scraped up the cost of building the trap in the first place, are so damn nosy. They are liable to come right down to your boat when you come in and look at the wounds so you have to poke them in all different places or it might look unnatural. Life keeps getting harder all the time.

Let us get back, for a moment, to the more authorized method of retrieving the traps. It is a common practice to leave a baited line overboard when the retrieval is being done. Experience has taught that large predators will often follow the trail of dislodged scales and traces of blood made by a pot full of panicked small fish all the way to the surface and, when this interesting collection suddenly vanishes into the air above, the frustrated toothy predator will grab anything that looks like a remnant meal. That's when you get to hook him on your line that you have prepared for this eventuality.

Sometimes it works like that. Usually it does but nothing is one hundred percent certain.

On one famous occasion, while taking a big trap into his canoe, the pot owner reached overboard to grasp the end of the frame to complete the tipping action that finally puts the wire mesh cage aboard only to find that a white tip shark, which had been lying in wait beneath the boat for any tasty offering, took him by the hand in the most literal sense of the phrase. Seeing exactly what the situation was, the other crewman then got a firm hold on the free arm and a vigorous bout of tug-o-war began. White tips have pretty good dentition so this only lasted a few minutes. It lasted till the shark managed to take the hand and about six inches of forearm away with him as a consolation prize. Forever after this the victim had to employ a third, two-handed worker to assist with the pot hauling which, as everyone knows, is extravagance. Yet another difficulty in practicing this way of making a living.

Back in the eighties, one of the outboard engine

manufacturers came out with a line of white propellers to distinguish their product from the black ones used by all the other competitors. Eventually people who bought these motors for use in the fish trap trade took to painting the propellers black after a few engines got torn off the backs of small boats. Although the engine would be in neutral while the trap hauling was going on, it seems that the current would slowly turn the white propeller, making it look like a dead or dying fish rolling over and over. Difficult to tell exactly what the fascination of it was, but that was the general theory. One minute you had an engine and the next a shark had it. A little change of ownership like that brings another new hardship in the life of the poor old fisherman, whose lot is said to be an empty gut and a wet behind.

"You ever seen one that big?" Louis asked. The young fellow put the giant barracuda down on the concrete floor of the fish room at the Co-Op.

Nobody had. A big specimen of this species might

grow up to thirty pounds in our waters. This one had just weighed in at sixty-two.

"Took it just as we did get the pot in. Thought it was a shark when the line start to fly." He showed them where the line had cut him and that was something quite impressive because a pot hauler has skin on his hands like shoe leather. "You think him have poison?"

It was a real worry with barracuda when they attain great size. There are ways of supposedly testing the wholesomeness of the flesh—like offering it to ants to see if they will eat it and boiling a piece in a pot of water with a silver spoon immersed and seeing if the silver turns black. Different people had various opinions about the efficacy of these methods. Sometimes they worked, sometimes they didn't. This poison seldom kills people but they are likely to wish they were dead for a long time after it hits them. Apart from the usual symptoms of vomiting and diarrhea, you can get odd reactions like cold water in your mouth feeling boiling hot and pains in your joints that last for months, even years.

The poison is called *ciguatera* and is now known
to reside in the skin, connective tissue, and flesh of fish
that graze on particular algae that covers coral.
Particularly dead coral. Lots of that around nowadays.
Especially since the spear fishermen have taken to
pushing bottles of chlorine bleach way up into the center
of a coral outcrop and breaking it. This drives the
crayfish out from the shelter of their rocky retreat and
they get to wipe out the whole population of that spot
instead of having to just shoot a few before they all go
deep into the crevices, which preserved them before this
marvelous discovery about the bleach. So efficient! And,
even though the chemical unfortunately kills the living
coral, there's lots of it about. There must be. It's always
been here.

The feeders that ingest the poison in the algae,
which now coats these bleached, ocean floor,
gravestones, are all small fish and very seldom contain
enough of the toxin to cause an adverse reaction in a
human. But flesh eaters, of which the barracuda is an

example near to the top of the food chain, eat a lot of these plant lovers over the years and accumulate the toxin. And the barracuda is very territorial so, if the particular area where he resides contains mostly dead coral, the chance of a large one carrying the poison goes up. And, since we can buy bleach anywhere, the whole place will soon be nothing but a flourishing algae garden. Then we will have to move on and get to work on deeper reefs further away. There's always a way out. It's sustainability, third-world style. Anybody got any ideas (and cash to back them up) that can change that?

A well-dressed little entourage drove up to the steps of the Co-Op building. A respectful crowd was gathered waiting. The visit was expected.

The old Member of Parliament, who had been the long time representative for the parish, had been laid low by an obesity-related cardiac catastrophe and a by-election had been scheduled to fill the vacancy. The hopeful candidate was one of the new breed, young and slim for the moment, and had been picked by national executives at party headquarters in Kingston and told to go and let the country dimwits get a look at him and tell them what they wanted to hear. "Remember respect for the old timers still goes a long way inside those communities out in the bush," the party directorship had told him. "They believe in that. Funny types, but there it is."

Mr. James went down the three steps to greet the candidate. "Come with me sir."

A podium had been constructed using six fish crates. Jimmy had left them out in the sun for three days and now they hardly smelled at all. At least, not to him. The candidate gave the "Fishing Beach Speech" to the group and asked for any questions.

"Are we going to be able to get flare guns to take to sea soon?"

"Of course," said the candidate, "I'll take care of it right after the election. That will be no problem."

"Gasoline is awful expensive," said another one.

"I am going to see that a subsidy is placed on all fishermen's fuel," promised the candidate. "I know there is one now but I will double the size of it. You can count on me!"

He cleared up a few more issues like that easily. "I am an advocate of change," he announced, like all hopefuls. That's usually a good idea. Everybody wants change because, after all, there's always something wrong and we want that changed. So everybody wants change we can believe in.

Everyone seemed to think he was just the man for the job. He could feel it. He began to feel a real love for these courteous, friendly people. Salt of the earth. So open and hospitable.

"Where are you going next?" Mr. James asked when the performance was over.

"I'm going to all three towns in this vicinity," said the candidate. "We're staying in a villa near the big hotel tonight. We stopped there this morning and my secretary —," he indicated to a fine specimen of Kingstonian womanhood who had sat behind him on the improvised stage while he was speaking, holding a scented handkerchief to her nose, "—was very pleased with how the place was set up. Modern kitchen. She is an excellent cook among many things and I'm rather hoping that we will get some fresh fish for dinner. Could we buy some here, sir?"

"Hold on a minute. Let me give you some. Please, as a present. How many of you? Three?" Mr. James looked to Michael, who went and cut six slices from Louis's big fish for the candidate's party. "Absolutely on the house. Compliments of The Fish House." Mr. James was a great believer in the lubrication supplied by mild humor and practiced it on all appropriate occasions.

Mr. James enquired from the caretaker at the villa in the morning.

"Ambulance had to come for them, boss! Them could hardly walk!"

*Well*, he thought, *they'll probably get over it. Most*

*people do.*

"Bad news, Louis," he told the young fisherman later. "You going to have to dump it. I tested it."

"Maybe the test not right, suh," Louis was still hopeful. "People tell me all the time that the poison tests —them is not reliable. Maybe you never do it right."

"I promise you, Louis," Mr. James told the still hopeful novice. "I know how to do it. Some tests are perfect."

# THE VILLAGE CURTAIN

# THE INVESTOR

The old Land Rover stopped on a grassy rise overlooking the western sweep of the bay. From here Mr. James could just see the small fishing village a few miles to the west and the big hill further away. In the morning breeze the broken surface of the ocean was filled with random, winking whitecaps. Dark patches moved over the lighter colored water near the beach where the clear sand shone through the water. These were schools of pilchards and they looked almost black under the surface, so dense were the concentrations. From time to time they would burst upward, showing their true silver color. They were jumping to escape the mackerel and small sennett barracuda that occasionally rushed at them from below.

Pelicans and terns, circling above them, yelled at each other hoping to insult the other competing species away from these lively, airborne breakfasts.

Mr. James got out of the vehicle and looked meaningfully at Michael, who seemed to be a bit slow to remember his instructions. Michael moved immediately upon receiving the quick glance and was at the front passenger door before the lady could get out and he slipped the battered, tricky lock upward and held it open for her to alight. He was not exactly used to this sort of thing but was familiar with the concept of salesmanship. Even the visitor looked slightly surprised at this gesture, which was vanishing all over the world, but she seemed pleased.

"The land goes from just in front of where we parked and all the way to where those black rocks come out into the sea near the stream and it extends back and north to the road," Mr. James said. "It's just over twelve acres. The guy from Kingston told me you wanted to put up about twenty villas and it would be more than enough.

You could leave all of those big trees in between the houses. He showed me the plans. If it were the way it looked on the drawing it would certainly be very nice. I don't want it getting sold to some big hotel project after I'm dead. What made you want to do it here though? We're a bit out of the way."

"I visited here, you know," said the lady, who was barely on the young side of middle age, but looked quite youthful. "The first time was just for a holiday but the second time was more of an investigation as to what was possible here. My husband did the layout that you saw. By then he knew he was not going to live much longer so he did this as a sort of dream thing. He never said a great deal about it but I think that was what it was."

That squared with what the realtor had said to Mr. James over the phone but Mr. James liked to hear things for himself. "A middle aged widow with cash, Cap'n James. How do you like that? A Mrs. Robert Carpenter from California. She's not going to come and muck up your precious outskirts. What the hell you ever do with that piece of grass anyway? Raise a few goats?"

Mr. James had another question for her. "Do you plan to live here?"

"That's really the point. The whole development is actually a sort of excuse, I guess. I mean—a justification," said Sonia Carpenter. "But I'm going to need a lot of advice on how things work on an extremely local level. I know how small communities can feel about outsiders. I don't want to have an awkward time with the building and so on. I'm going to have to find someone from right here to be with me and help me along right from the very start. Is there anybody like that you could recommend? Someone who I could think of as almost a partner. Not a financial partner. I understand that. A partner in other ways."

"Mikey, here works for me, but I think he's getting bored. He grew up here and is a sort of relative of mine." He was on the verge of saying that Michael had actually lived in Miami but that was a slightly awkward period so he decided that he could tell her himself, eventually, if things worked out that way. Michael had walked down to the shoreline and was standing near the water with the dog that had traveled out with them in the back seat. The dog was really getting old now and preferred to sit and watch the birds diving in the surf rather than chase after them in the shallows as he had once done. He had reached a contemplative age and had been faced with making several adjustments along the way.

"Of course I wouldn't expect you to just take him on immediately or anything like that, Mrs. Carpenter," continued Mr. James in his slightly old-fashioned, formal way. "Naturally it would depend on if we agreed on a cost and, in any case, you would have to get to know him."

"Well, I'm looking forward to that. And please— call me Sonia. I just know we're all going to be the best of friends."

Mr. James waved to Michael who came back across the sand with the wind behind him; walking toward them, the old dog keeping up very well anticipating the ride home. The airflow was increasing slightly all the time as the heat of the morning lifted the atmospheric pressure over the warming land.

*The smell of the place and the people are a big part of it,* Sonia thought. *Oh God, in whom I have trouble even believing, forgive me, as I have asked you before—but the smell of death was sometimes too much for me and I would have to say, "I'll be right back. The nurse is right here. I'll be back straight away." I have always been affected powerfully by scent. I was so ashamed of it all those months but I could not help it. I wanted to stay there but I just couldn't—not constantly.* She shook her head, trying to drive away the memory. They say you can't really remember smells at will and maybe that's true but you can remember what they did to you. *I just couldn't help it.*

Sonia breathed as deeply as she could, filling her lungs with the life of the rushing, ozone laden, salt-impregnated air.

In the town of Black River they drove very slowly along the main street because that is the only way you can drive there at all. Every type of conveyance jostled for space. Donkeys and bicycles faced down trucks. Handcarts challenged taxis. Along the sidewalks, vendors with portable stands offered everything from cutlery to cuisine, forced pedestrians into the street, adding to the congestion. The cooking stalls competed fiercely and the crowd-smell blended with the aroma of curry, pimento, smoke, and other, more complex, mixtures. The old Land Rover admitted all of this rich third-world bouquet freely, every remaining window being pulled open to help contend with the heat.

Sonia shook her head and felt almost intoxicated. *They should bottle it.* The old dog in the back, sitting on a discarded coat that Mr. James had worn for twenty years, lifted his head appreciatively. Time had clouded his eyes a little and corroded his joints, his digestion was somewhat impaired from his drinking years, but he was as keen a connoisseur of this familiar olfactory banquet as he had ever been.

"You want me to stop and get you a bite to eat, Mrs. Carpenter?" Mr. James had not quite got to the Sonia stage yet. "That fellow over there does very good barbecue chicken. Jerked fish too."

"Anything. Anything at all. Everything smells wonderful."

The dog seemed very pleased. He couldn't understand a word the lady said in her unusual accent but he had caught the *stop* and *eat* part in the well-known cadence of Mr. James and these struck him as very fine ideas indeed.

Michael leaned forward to speak while they waited for Mr. James to get back. "Is not everyone who can live here, Sonia," he said. He was far less formal than Mr. James.

"Oh, but I have been here before, you know," she said. "I know all about the sand flies and the mosquitoes and so on. I used to make jokes about them."

"You going to have to make lots of jokes to live

here."

# THE VILLAGE CURTAIN

# THE INVESTOR REFLECTS

I got a lot out of it.

First of all there was getting to know the people. Well, as far as I could. Then the unbelievable chaos and inefficiency that would have made Robert, argumentative but oh so gentle Robert, go completely nuts. God how he *hated* bureaucracy! And all along the way there were "little men" who had to get a present for providing some stamp that was absolutely vital to the project. Men who could apply larger stamps had to receive more substantial inducements. These people were referred to as "big men" to match the grandeur of their stamps.

Then, although there were miles of sand—it was sea sand. You had to get river sand for building because of the salt. That was a big problem for it had to be trucked from who knows where. Its origin seemed to be something of a local secret. I hope it was legal. Or, at least, fairly legal.

Everyone in Kingston warned me that if you left so much as a shovel unattended on the site for five minutes it might get stolen but that never happened to me. I think, I honestly think, the people of the district did not dislike me. They were just reserved. I was from outside, but I never felt any hostility or resentment and Mike helped with that a great deal. And Mr. James, to tell the truth, probably even more, although I never quite got past his vaguely distant style. He had a way of answering you after a slight pause and I believe he considered even the smallest matter with caution. He knew a lot of things but he disclosed them in a most careful, guarded manner.

Watching it all grow was fun too and I had this sense that in some way I was doing it for Robert, and that emotion grew stronger as time passed and got in the way of other feelings, till I was afraid that I was becoming almost morbid sometimes and thought, *Come off it—it's not a cemetery, you fool. It's going to be a beautiful place where hundreds and hundreds of people will be happy forever, and maybe me too.* I would shake it off and go and sit by the sea and we would talk about little local, inside-type things and I would get to know bits of stories about what went on. Also, sometimes, about things that had happened in the past. I knew instinctively that some of the stories were edited because I was still an outsider, to some extent, and always would be.

I used to go up to the big hill with the lighthouse and I could see the buildings, very tiny in the distance. I would sit and look out for hours but Mike told me that it was a place with bad history and not a "good" place so, after a while, I used to go there almost in secret because it did have an odd attraction for me. Once I took the old dog with me and he wouldn't go near the edge where I liked to sit. I believe it is a strange place and it alters your perspective and maybe it is a spot with an addictive effect like other mind-altering things. It makes things look so disproportionate.

I remember the early morning in late August, when I went out on the first totally completed balcony of what was going to be my house. The wood of the floor was damp underfoot with the morning dew and I could smell the wet lumber. The morning was picture-perfect with the light slanting off the water and Mike came up behind me with his little battery radio and said, "Listen to this." It was the tail end of a weather report about a hurricane that had crossed over the Windward Islands two days ago and was expected to pass south of Jamaica as a medium sized storm. Looking around, it seemed like news about something happening in another world. I made some silly, first-thing-in-the-morning crack about hurry up hurricane or something like that but he seemed concerned and said no hurricane was a joke, especially to the south.

The next morning, Frankie came with a huge

truck and the fellows put the boats in it, lifting canoes that must have weighed a half a ton by pure manpower. They made several trips inland. The day was as lovely as ever with the usual sea breeze cooling the skin of the half-naked men loading the truck. They called out to each other during the work, but with less laughter and more urgency than normal.

That night, it fell deathly quiet and I got up at about two in the morning and Mike was sitting on the step and he said, "Listen. "

I said, "To what?"

"That's the problem."

The ever-present song of the frogs was missing. In the morning the bird calls were not there, not even the sea birds, but the swell was rolling in and building although there was not a whisper of wind. The tide was higher than I had ever seen it. There was a lot of confusion about the hurricane now with reports that a plane had centered it about fifty miles further north than the estimated position. Also something about wind shear being totally absent over the system so there was nothing to contain or inhibit its rapid strengthening.

About an hour before sunset, Mr. James came up to the house and said something to Mike. Then he came over to me and said, " Miss Sonia, " that's as far as he ever managed to progress with informality, "Please come with us. I have a small house in the mountains. It's not anything much, but it is in a hollow and no tall trees near. You must not stay here." I could not quite grasp all of it even then. It was almost breathless weather, just a tiny draught from the west, which is the rarest of wind directions in this island, and the dull roar of the unusually discordant swell.

I was a bit surprised to hear about this mountain house. Another insider secret that you get to find out apparently on a strictly need-to-know basis.

When we got there it looked like a glorified shack. Nothing near as substantial as the solid villa I had left. But the mountains surrounded it on all sides and the sky was only a huge circle above. In the last of the light the high clouds were scurrying past now but it was very still in this pocket.

"This is Eva," Mr. James said by way of introduction to the buxom young woman who came out. Eva nodded and smiled with her lips pressed together. Mike helped me with the luggage. Mr. James left us, expressing a formal regret that he must get back to his own house before conditions got any worse.

I had expected that up here in the forest there would have been bird whistles and insect chirping and woodland-type background noise but it was deathly silent as the light faded. I asked Mike about that and he said, "They know when it's coming."

That night the three of us stayed in the "big room" that seemed to be a combination of kitchen, dining and sitting place. There was no electricity up here in the forest, but Eva had a Tilley lamp that ran on kerosene and it was bright and radiated heat. After a while, I talked with Eva and she seemed to thaw out and suddenly she said, "Me did think you was younger," then clapped her hand over her mouth and laughed. I think she was self conscious about her front teeth, or lack thereof.

The sounds from outside were truly awful but through the screaming of the wind above you could hear when a big tree fell. Even in this well sheltered place, there was plenty of swirling updraft air. Twice Mike had to go outside in the wild, horizontal rain and do things to zinc sheets on the roof that were coming loose. It seemed funny that there was no lightning to add to the drama but I learned later that in the thick of a big hurricane people on the ground seldom see that because the visibility is almost zero. I put my hand on the old dog and he was trembling.

"Has he ever been through one of these?" I asked.

Eva said, "Not like this one."

The next day there was no question about getting back down the road by which we had ascended. It was only a half road to begin with. But the day after that Frankie came to tell us that Mr. James had made it to within about a mile of us. If I wanted to walk to where he was so as to get back down I could come. Mr. James' home was only slightly damaged, being far back from the shore behind the small sheltering escarpment. He said that it had flooded but was okay now. He mentioned that I could stay there for a while if I wanted. When I asked him why he said, "I will show you," and twenty minutes later I understood.

There was utterly nothing left of the sixteen nearly completed villas and the two almost finished ones.

Well, that's not quite true, of course. You could see where they had been, by foundations and the occasional lonely concrete column, but the sea had put the land surface back pretty much the way it had been when I first saw it. The big trees were all torn up to some extent but only two were uprooted. I couldn't believe it but, after a while, I had to.

I got home to L.A. a week later and now, when I think about it, the whole thing has a dream-like quality about it. It had started as a dream, even though it had not been mine, but I had let it interfere with my mind till I caught it like some sort of mental influenza. Breathed it in, I think. As contagious and impractical as love and dreams usually are.

I still own the land so I suppose there's something real left. Mr. James rented it from me and I believe he has a big herd of goats on it now. Next year I'm going to go back and stay at his house and see all the people who became special to me. I'll go and sit out on the high place to see, off in the distance, the clear, tree-spotted land where the dream was supposed to come alive, and smell the ocean wind, confident that it will always be there if I need it, and know that even though there's no structure as a monument to the adventure, I did something once in my life that was absolutely impractical in all sorts of ways.

That's why I still think I got a lot out of it.

# A QUIET, RAINY NIGHT IN THE MOUNTAINS

His earliest memories were of the fine, white coral sand and the warm sea. He learned to walk on the one and swim in the other almost at the same time. He would play where these two elements met and his brothers and sisters would always be with him, testing his strength, speed, and daring in the shifting border of the water and the land, constantly changing the rules of the endless tag game to suit the varying conditions that the wind and the tide would create. The youngsters drove themselves to healthy exhaustion daily. Their mother would sit, sensibly, back in the shade where the first line of trees

137

grew, in that place where the powdery beach transitioned to rich earth, watching over them proudly. She was a mother of much experience and enjoyed an excellent reputation in the village. All her children did not share a common father but that was traditional too. So he grew up like the others and everything was simple.

But *love*, as the song goes, *changes everything.*

The day she came into his life everything changed. He was enveloped in his adoration to the point that nothing in the world was ever the same again. So devoted did he become that not even other recipients of her affection ever made the slightest difference to him. He simply welcomed these as joyful additions to their circle. Anything that made her happy made him happy too.

*Love, love changes everything . . .*

So when he lost her, finally and completely, nothing in this world was ever quite the same. Like other abandoned lovers before him, he drowned his sorrows for a while in the tolerance of the barroom, but other love came along, not the same kind of thing of course, but infinitely better than the aimless drift of the drunkard. And, coming as he did from a long line of survivors, he made out okay, as they say.

On this late midsummer's afternoon, with the unmistakable smell of an approaching evening shower strong in the air, he walked up the familiar gentle incline across the clearing, climbed the few worn steps to his home and, out of nowhere, there came a weariness that engulfed him and was such as he had never known. It was all he could do to barely acknowledge the greeting from his family before he lay down and tried to breathe normally after that small effort. And the darkness fell around the cabin, a very gentle rain along with it.

The sounds of the household faded in his ears. His heartbeat slowed and he half slept, then slept truly, in the safety and comfort of being under a sound roof, while the rain drummed on and the cool wind from the highest slopes whispered outside. He began to dream of the beach, something that had not happened for as long as he could remember. The scene floated in and out of focus and suddenly he saw her clearly, as he had seen her in his youth, with her brilliant smile and her arms were open to him and she said, as she had done so long ago, "Come with me, friend," and he went with her, happily, into her world forever.

"What's wrong with him?" said Mr. James. He was sitting at the table with a glass of coconut water in front of him. Michael, who had noticed the strange silence, went over and put his hand against the still warm body. Then he put his finger to his own mouth, moistened it, and put it near the blunt nose and said quietly, "He's dead. Him was pretty old."

"Well . . ." said Mr. James. He seemed to have run out of anything further to add by way of commentary.

The door of the cottage was wide open. The wet woodland smell came freely into the room along with the sounds of the forest at night. Michael stepped out onto to the porch and said, "It's stopped raining. Eva, bring the shovel."

"Where are you going to bury him, Mikey?"

"Out the back, with the others."

"Mikey," Mr. James said, "That's a family plot. Your own mother and your sister—them is buried there. Eva's two uncles as well. My own wife says she wants to go back there to sleep, as she calls it. For God's sake don't tell her if this is what you going to do. It would kill her. You want to put *her* to sleep?" Mr. James knew just how far to take a joke but, also, how necessary to perspective it can be.

The three of them walked to where a huge cotton tree spread its black umbrella above them. Half a dozen simple stone monuments were scattered about in the vicinity. The leaves overhead dripped steadily upon the little funeral party. Mr. James carried the hissing Tilley lamp. Strong Eva was holding the old dog gently across her breast as though pretending that, even in death, he could still feel her embrace. His broad head was cradled on her shoulder. Michael easily drove the spade into the damp, soft, accommodating earth. He dug a small grave near a concrete slab that was neatly chiseled with just the name *Myra*.

"Listen Mikey," said Mr. James. "Seriously now. You not going to put a marker or anything like that here are you? Tell me that."

"Don't worry. I won't need anything to help me remember where he is."

# THE BEACH FISHERMAN

Weather plays a part in every kind of hunting but it is more critical in certain endeavors than others. The particular method practiced by Leo required calm conditions in the last hour of daylight. Small surf was another desirable contributor, as the mullet had a tendency to ride the incoming swell in the time before sunset and, with the failing light behind you, their forms were visible through the concave wall of the incoming surf as if they were racing along the side of a curved glass wall.

These fish have another peculiar trait that works in the favor of the rare type of harvester in which Leo considered himself an expert. That is to say he was reasonably accomplished, as far as one can become, in a skill that involved the employment of equipment in a way for which it was never designed to be used. This fishy peculiarity is an inordinate curiosity, which makes them circle and investigate a small concentrated disturbance on the surface, bunching together as they do so. To take advantage of this response, Leo would throw a small stone into the water close to the patrolling school. Instead of continuing with their rush parallel to the beach, the group would turn and close in on the spot where the splash had occurred and thus congregate briefly in a small area. That was how Leo needed them to present themselves, even if it was only for a few seconds.

Leo was a dynamiter.

This is not a type of fishing generally approved by the readers of *Field & Stream*, nor is it a technique which lends itself to those dedicated to the principle of catch and release. It is also frowned upon by scrupulous officers attached to various law enforcement units. Most countries do not encourage their private, informally trained citizens to blow fish up with dynamite as they feel that the possession of this explosive material should be regulated, restricted, and handled only by professionals who are trained to keep it under strict control and documented supervision.

Leo kept his supplies tightly wrapped in grease paper in a thick plastic bag underneath a chicken house in his backyard where dogs, children and goats roamed and played. Once again, this type of storage would have raised a few eyebrows in official quarters but was a perfectly secure piece of private village intelligence. His father, who initiated him into this art, had kept his sticks there and only brought them inside his house if a hurricane or major flood was expected. Therefore, maintaining the location was a family tradition and respected as such.

Leo's father never had an accident directly attributable to his special trade. He went to his grave with all his extremities attached in their original arrangement, which is rare in this type of employment, but it was generally agreed that he died from a work-related handicap. He was run over by a car that was admittedly going very quickly but had announced its progress with a loud horn. Everybody agreed that a man who had even basic hearing would not have attempted to cross the main road at that particular moment, but Leo's father had damaged his ability to discern anything much softer than a detonation that he had personally engineered.

Deafness is a regular by-product of proximity to very loud noises. In a dynamiter of fish, where the distance from the explosion is not great, this kind of development is a career-affiliated hazard. Ideally, the noise ought to be reasonably contained as the blast should occur just *below* the surface to have the desired effect, and the sound is somewhat muffled. Only a mistimed detonation is really very loud. But fuses are temperamental and there are other features to this fishing that can cause departures from the program.

Dynamite is not cheap especially considering that,

if you do not possess the right qualifications, you have to pay a premium price to some construction contractor or road builder for the trouble he must take confusing the records as to where and when it was used. So part of the technique involves keeping a keen eye on the fish and pinching off the wick if they begin to disperse before you think you can ensnare them. If you pinch off the wick behind where the burn has progressed there may be only the few fractions of a second warning from the still hissing device to get rid of it. If that happens, the whole affair gets extremely problematical and any distance away from the point of ignition is to be gained urgently if at all possible. A lot depends on it. In the event that this happens with any frequency, the minimum side effect is some degree of hearing impairment. As that handicap progresses, the likelihood of noticing the fatal hiss of the still-burning fuse increases and, consequently, so does the possibility of a truly unpleasant event.

On a quiet late afternoon in August, Leo was slowly

walking along the beach heading east with the light of the setting sun sharp on the still shining surface of the sea. He stayed just out of the reach of the actual wavelets to keep the whole scene as natural as possible. A mile from the village, he came upon Frankie who was going the other way. Frankie had a bag over his shoulder and a lamp made from a bottle filled with kerosene and with a wick forced into the mouth. He was heading towards the grasslands that bordered the swamp where he could catch big land crabs.

"Some of them is just past the rocks," Frankie said. "Two bodies of them. Quite a few."

"That's where they always like," Leo said. "Topside the rocks?"

"Yes, man. Right near in."

"All right, Frankie."

Leo felt quietly confident. If the mullet were really close to the rocky outcrop it was possible to stand on the promontory and get an extra few feet of advantage both upward and seaward. This was a spot where he had done well in the past, but it was especially nice to have this advance notice. He considered promising Frankie two mullet but decided not to do so in case it was all fantasy. Fishermen lie to each other quite routinely to keep the art alive. It gave you the opportunity to say something like this: "You didn't see any? You losing your skill. Them was plenty there. Big ones, for true!"

The rocks went about twenty feet out into the sea and right beside them there was an underground spring of fresh water that came up through the sea floor and made the water muddy and colder than the surrounding section. It was a place favored by surf dwelling species. Armed with this probably accurate advance information, Leo advanced very carefully onto the stony platform.

He could see them now. One big school with maybe twenty fish at the very point of the encroaching bar of stone and the other, slightly smaller, group a few yards further out.

Leo picked up two small stones and made ready. There was still plenty of light. When they were in the vicinity of the rocks, the fish bunched, separated, and reformed in a more random manner than they did along the beach. It was a favorite haunt of wandering schools but it had its own particular difficulties.

Jimmy put a cold beer in front of newly, officially promoted Mr. Anderson. "There you are, Chief," he said. What could he call him now? *Senior Superintendent* sounded odd. He had called him *Superintendent* when he was an inspector and, therefore, logic dictated that he ought to award his own brand of rural courtesy to this distinguished son of the village and bring him up a notch. But all the next grades sounded awkward. *Senior Superintendent?* Hardly. So, for the moment, till he had solved this knotty problem of etiquette, he decided that *Chief* was the best he could think of.

"I hear you have a new boss, Roy," said Mr. James.

"That's right. Imagine an Englishman. On loan from Scotland Yard."

"How do you like him?"

"He has a mouth as big as a sunfish—but he's not as smart." The so-called Caribbean sunfish is a local name for a perch-like fish with an enormous maw that takes up position a few inches below the surface wherever he finds a floating object or a patch of grass. He is so sluggish and unwitting that even the most incompetent angler can scoop him up with a dip net. Hence he is called the savior of the foolish fisherman, who would die of hunger if there were not so dim a creature.

"Everyday he has a press conference," said Mr. Anderson. "He told the newspaper that he did not come here to solve crime. So the reporter asked him how come his position is Deputy Commissioner in charge of crime and he said he's a consultant. So I thought he should be Deputy Consultant but they don't have that post in the force and being a foreigner they could hardly make him anything less than some sort of commissioner."

"What about Commissioner Sunfish?"

Everyone, except Mr. James who stuck to his usual coconut water, had drunk quite a bit of rum so it was easy to be humorous.

"It's getting dark, Jimmy. What about some light in here? I want to see what I'm drinking," Mr. Anderson said.

There was a loud bang from down the beach.

"Leo," said Jimmy.

Mr. James went to the door and looked down the length of the bay. "I don't see anybody," he said. There was still plenty of light outside.

"It sounded pretty close," said a Pedro Cay fisherman from the end of the bar.

"It was too loud," said Mr. James. "I'm going to take a look."


Dr. Mitchell was the resident medical officer at the Black River hospital. He regarded it as a hardship post and thought that the health authorities held his high achievement record at university against him. Dr.

Mitchell believed that he was a very intelligent young physician and disliked every single thing about the rural nature of the facility in which he found himself. Only the strictures of a student loan held him in thrall of government service.

Dr. Mitchell stood beside the bed and asked, "How are you doing, Leo?"

"All right. Me still feel like the hand is there." Leo looked down to at his right wrist, where his hand used to be. All that remained was white bandage wrapped around the bottom of his forearm.

"That's how it goes," Dr Mitchell said with a cheerful smile. "Everybody says that." He sounded as if he treated people whose hands had been blown off every day.

"Me still no hear so good."

"That may get better to some extent, Leo. Of course it may not. You could go stone deaf in a little while. Yes, come to think of it, that is quite likely. In any case, I guess your days with the dynamite are over. I

heard all about it from the men who brought you here."
Dr. Mitchell had a bedside manner that lacked empathy.
Only the relatively greater misery of his patients made his
days in this contemptible backwater bearable. Something
else occurred to him, which he thought it would be nice
to pass on to his patient. "A policeman came by asking
about you yesterday. Maybe you have some more trouble
coming your way. A superintendent named Anderson."

Leo knew that was okay. But the hand was a
problem. After all, you had to throw the congregating
stone as well as hold, and then light, the charge. Anyway
you looked at it *that* was a problem.

Michael came along the beach. He was carrying a bundle
of staves made from black mangrove. These are used to
make the frames of the fish traps. He had gone back far in
the swamp to cut them for Louis where the big, straight
ones were still to be found. He stopped short of the rocky
promontory when he saw the familiar figure of Leo out
on the end of the little stony point. It looked like Leo was

lining up for a try at his old profession but only three weeks ago he had been in the hospital and everybody knew that, as the village wit put it, he was short-handed now.

Michael saw when Leo threw the stone a few feet out into the quiet water. On the surface, the trails of the concentrating school were quite clear. Then Michael saw how the new plan was going to work. As soon as he tossed the pebble with his good left hand, Leo struck the match and lit the stick, which he was holding in his mouth like a giant cigar. Then he took the fizzing explosive from his lips and tossed it left-handed at the center of the swirling group of fish.

The two of them waded into the shallow water and began to pick up the mullet together, putting them into Leo's big mesh bag that was tied to his waist.

"You practice it first?" Michael asked him.

"For true," said Leo. "You think me is a fool? You can make a mistake with a hand or a foot but you only got one head."

# THE VILLAGE CURTAIN

# HOOKED

A few weeks later, Leo went back to Dr. Mitchell for a check-up.

"It has healed very well indeed," Dr Mitchell said. "How's the hearing?"

"Good, Doc. Me hear good."

"And thanks for the fish, Leo. You got a new way of making a living now?"

"Yes, Doc. Me is never going to touch that stuff again."

"You know I never went fishing in my life."

"You want to go, Doc? Me can ask my friend Mikey. He would take you out for a little trip. Just a few hours. Maybe you like it. When you want to go?"

Dr. Mitchell wasn't sure he wanted to go at all but he was so bored he told Leo that, if he could arrange it, he would drive down to the village on Saturday morning. "But just for a little while, you understand. I have to be on duty in the afternoon."

This was not strictly true but he was already preparing his exit strategy. He thought it might be faintly interesting to go just once. Then he could say, "I went fishing with those guys when I was stuck down in the wilderness, you know. God, what a bunch of primitives they are." Something like that would sound fine at a party in the suburbs of Kingston, where the young professionals gather to impress each other.

Which was how he came to be standing, with his bare feet in cold seawater, holding onto the gunwale of a skiff while Michael put a pail and a few other items into the doubtful-looking little boat. He was feeling slightly foolish as we often do when we are in unfamiliar situations. In his particular case, he especially did not relish being in a junior capacity to someone whom he was perfectly sure was his social and intellectual inferior in every way. It was almost chilly in the dawn and he was concentrating on not shivering because the last thing on the earth he wanted to convey was that he was frightened. Suddenly he began to think along those lines.

"How far are we going?"

"Just in the bay," Michael promised.

That didn't sound so bad. The doctor thought the diminutive twenty-five horsepower engine sounded as rough as it looked. Dr. Mitchell was uneasy to observe that no oars or paddles were part of the onboard equipment of the vessel but thought a comment on this would be out of place. As the boat cleared the headland, the sun broke free from the surface of the eastern sea-rim and, for a few moments, you could look straight into its glowing half eye. It was a new experience for the doctor.

Michael took a silver fish, which looked like a big herring with a beak, from the bucket and threaded a hook through the mouth and out of the body just in front of the anal fin. The hook was attached to a few feet of stainless steel wire then clipped with a swivel to a thick nylon line. This line was wrapped on a wooden spool. Michael let out about twenty yards of the line and handed it to Dr. Mitchell.

"You want a glove?" Michael asked.

There were two worn and battered-looking, leather gloves in the bucket along with the bait. He offered one to the doctor. Pungent, red water dripped from its fingers. Dr. Mitchell looked at this object suspiciously. "Do you think I need it?"

"No. Maybe not. In here them about ten pound size or so. Sometimes you get a big one. Hardly ever this late in the year. You'd have to be lucky."

Dr. Mitchell held the line and felt a constant, uneven throb. "How come it feels like it's shaking all the time?"

"Me rig it like that. Bend the head down a bit before me tie it to the wire so it makes the dead bait-fish wag and look like it not feeling well or got some damage done to it. The kingfish look for an injured fish to kill. Them is always cleaning up the place. No sick fish live long round here. Kingfish kill them if them not strong." *Like doctors*, he thought, but he kept the joke to himself. He was doing Leo a favor and was far from sure if this medical person had the rare ability to laugh at himself.

The sun was clear of the horizon now but still not able to totally defeat the coolness of the morning. Dr. Mitchell was pleasantly surprised at how well he felt in the sharp, briny air. He was thinking of the advice he gave many of his patients when he had worked in Kingston, about getting up early and going for a walk, might be really good for them. He did not feel the requirement to give this advice now that he had been exiled to this outpost of desolation in the countryside. Most of the people that he saw in this region, which he called "the place behind God's back," got up before daybreak anyway and didn't look like they were short of exercise. Perhaps other things, like proper education and soap.

It was peaceful but just a bit boring. The engine rattled unsteadily along, trailing a thin smoke line. Dr. Mitchell disliked the sound it made more and more as the distance from the shore increased.

"You make a living at this?" Dr. Mitchell asked to pass the time.

"Not this," Michael said. "Me just do this sometimes. Me work at the fish house and for Mr. James a bit."

"Your friend, Leo, he was a full-time fisherman though. Till he blew off his hand. What is he doing now?"

"Well," said Michael, "He helps out all round as best he can. Nobody round here don't fool with dynamite anymore."

"That's good. I thought he might be in even more problems when a policeman came round to the hospital while he was there but I haven't heard that anything came of it."

"Maybe they think he suffered enough. That and him giving up doing it. Me hear him throw away all the dynamite. Him could never do it anymore after what happened."

Looking astern, Dr. Mitchell saw two white seagulls circle and swoop down to the surface approximately the distance behind them where he guessed that the bait was submerged. At the same time a quantity of tiny, shining, sardine-like fish jumped in all directions, like a silvery fountain. The gulls went crazy, wheeling and trying to catch the leaping minnows in the air. There was a big swirl on the top of the calm surface. The birds hovered directly over it.

"Hold the line tight, Doc," said Michael. "Whatever happens no make it run through your fingers or it will burn you bad. Even cut you. Hold it tight."

Dr. Mitchell started to say that nothing had happened when he felt it. It was as though a very strong hand had suddenly grasped the other end of the line and was determined to wrench it away from his grasp. Suddenly he felt as though he was connected to the very heart of a primeval force that was engaged in some ancient life and death dispute.

Michael cut the motor to a dead idle. Some of the pressure came off the line but the angle kept changing all the time and Dr. Mitchell could only get a few yards when the fish let him.

"Suppose it breaks?" he asked. He felt that if that happened he could not bear it.

"It no can break," Michael said. "That line is one hundred fifty pound strain. Nothing inside here can break that. Just no let him get any slack. That's the way them get off. Them get slack line and throw the hook."

When the kingfish was within a few feet of the transom, Michael picked up the gaff and put the engine in neutral. Dr. Mitchell saw the fish for the first time, white and shining as it tried to turn broadside to the boat. Michael leaned over and, as the kingfish passed very close to the after corner of the skiff, put the hook of the landing gaff into a point just behind the head of the fish where it would do almost no damage to the usable flesh. He brought the kingfish aboard with one smooth lift, slipping the gaff out at the same moment that the fish hit the floor of the boat.

"Nice one," said Michael. "About twelve pounds. Big for inside here. You is a lucky fisherman."

Dr. Mitchell observed the fish, which was changing color by the second as waves of blue and silver chased each other along its body in response to the influx of oxygen in its blood supply. He thought it was the most beautiful thing he had ever seen. Even more beautiful than the medical certificate, which hung in its neat frame on his office wall and which he had hunted grimly through the years of study and stress at the university.

Dr. Mitchell looked south to where the wide bay merged into the open expanse of the Caribbean Sea. Out there the water was a deep indigo, marking where the island shelf fell away precipitously to depths of over a thousand feet. All along this line of color change flocks of birds were working. They were diving among the bursts of spray caused by the bait fish jumping amidst the splashes made by the predators as they came raging up to the surface zone where the small fish ran out of water room. A kingfish, traveling at full speed, was carried more than a yard into the air by the momentum of his rushing strike and shone, a brilliant, flashing arc, in the glancing sunlight. In the moment of the feeding frenzy, the surface was alive with the never-ending battle for survival. The marvel of it was that fifteen minutes earlier the surface had looked placid and only the occasional patrolling bird had been in sight.

"All sort of stuff around today. We call it a biting time. You can never tell when them will just start like that." Michael remarked. He was trying to sound as dispassionate as possible by way of courtesy to his passenger but he couldn't quite suppress his fisherman's instinct. "See them black man-o-war birds out there past the others? Tuna or dolphin is under them."

"Listen," Dr. Mitchell said. "If we go further outside like, far out, you know. Suppose we did that? You think we might get to catch a really big one? Give me the gloves. You did say the line could stand more than a hundred pounds. What you say, Mikey?"

Michael brought the bow of the boat around to where it pointed at the most concentrated section of the schooling fish. Dr. Mitchell held the line very firmly knowing now, armed with his insider's experience in these matters, how important that was. He could hear the cries of the birds as they passed information among themselves. He noticed, with satisfaction and without apprehension, the slightly louder slap of the wavelets as the protection of the bay's embrace fell away. He listened to the little engine. It sounded smoother to him now.

# THE VILLAGE CURTAIN

# PART 3

# THE VILLAGE CURTAIN

# MRS. CARPENTER MEETS THE CHARITY MAN

Sonia Carpenter finished her morning walk along what she called "her favorite piece of sand in the whole world" and climbed the gentle, grassy incline that led to the old, sprawling, zinc-sheet roofed, timber home of her friend Mr. James. The house was just visible from the beach because it was partly nestled behind a small, rocky foothill that curled around it like a protective arm. That feature had been worth a lot in safety for the dwelling on the occasions when nature threw a Caribbean summer tantrum and hurled the whole bay ashore to see if what was built within its reach could withstand that sort of test.

When she came in sight of the long front porch she was surprised to see that there was a visitor sitting at the big, smooth wooden table having coffee with Mr. James. The stranger was a new face to her and she had a tiny pride in believing that she knew every person who lived in the village. She had long since christened herself as an honorary insider. Mr. James, who was unfailingly carefully formal, rose and introduced her to the newcomer, who stood to greet her.

"Mrs. Carpenter, this is an old friend of mine. His name is Mr. Patrick. For many years he worked as a friend of our community and many others. We call him The Charity Man."

"Good morning, Mrs. Carpenter," said The Charity Man, who might have been Mr. something Patrick or, just as possibly, Mr. Patrick something. These subtle linguistic decisions were made at a level still incompressible to Sonia Carpenter, who came from a culture where everybody was less sensitive to such fine distinctions.

172

"Hi," said Sonia, playing as safe as possible. "How come they call you The Charity Man?" Everybody sat down again.

"I worked for an international Christian-based poor relief organization that concentrated a lot of its efforts in these islands. I had Jamaica, Haiti, Belize and the Dominican Republic as my territories."

"That must have been such rewarding work," said Sonia. "I bet you changed many lives for the better."

"Who knows," said The Charity Man. "I gave away a lot of stuff. I gave boats and engines to men who had cranky little skiffs that could hardly make it two miles offshore and later I saw pictures of them being arrested two hundred miles out to sea in the Windward Passage with a cargo of narcotics worth a half a million United States dollars or carrying a hundred automatic rifles in crates. I guess that changed their lives a whole lot."

There was a slightly awkward silence while everybody considered this response. Mr. James seemed to find the comments mildly amusing but Sonia looked like she thought it was a bit harsh.

"Surely that must have been the very rare exception."

"Oh yes," said The Charity Man. "Quite exceptional. Most of them never got caught at all. Anyway, the majority just stuck to stealing fish traps from the fellows that I never got around to giving good boats and engines. With the good new equipment, the ones I missed could never catch them. This too, changed people's lives."

"Mr. Patrick is a joker, Mrs. Carpenter. He likes to run these jokes all the time." Mr. James, the eternal voice of moderation, lowering the conversational temperature.

"It was a joke, all right. I would get a project together and really think it might fly the way I figured it and then it would develop a life of its own both in my organization and then on the ground and I couldn't recognize it after a while. Although my father came from England, I was born on this island you know, and I still

174

can't understand plenty of what goes on but I understand a lot and eventually I just decided to hell with it. You teach people to use GPS and even satellite phones and you get more efficient smugglers—but you get safety too. The truth is that there are only half truths and half measures. They have their inside secrets and they're welcome to them. I love them though. Some kind of way."

There it was again. The old inside/outside conundrum that Sonia always found at the heart of life in the village.

"Well," she said, "I believe it's the same in small, close-knit communities all over the world. It's a survival technique."

"Sure it is. And it's tighter than ever in a culture with a slave history, I believe that absolutely. It is even more intense in some places than here. Let me tell you a story . . ." The Charity Man leaned forward, crossing his arms over the table.

"I began doing a lot of work in a territory—not

Jamaica—way up in the mountains and there was this particular little town in a very isolated area. Only about ten people in the whole place had ever been more than a few miles from where they were born. I spent a lot of time with them. I believe I was the first man with a bit of a fat belly most of them had ever seen because they were all thin as rails. I'm pretty sure about this because the children started a rumor that, in my alien race, it was possible to be a pregnant man and all the little kids believed it for a while." He leaned back to reveal his round belly and gave it a few pats. Sonia giggled.

"Anyway, I got so that I really felt I was an insider in the truest sense and I even got to know that this village had a reputation for being able to hold the most pure ceremonies of what lots of people call voodoo. People with really deep pockets down in the capital would scrape up a big contribution and pay to have a genuine spellbinder or curse removal or hex installation cooked up there. It was about the only inflow of actual cash the priest and boss of the place ever saw. This was a big

176

secret business, you understand, illegal as hell, and there were grades of magnitude that had to do with the price and the problem requiring magical interventions. I saw several of them. They were quite impressive with chickens getting their heads bitten off and sheep being ritually disemboweled and gruesome stuff like that which seemed to satisfy the characters that were paying the bill. I was very proud of my status as an insider because I had been told that I was the first person not born on that island ever to have been accorded the privilege of attending something so intimate."

Now it was Sonia who leaned in closer, elbows on table.

"Well, I was over in a region about twenty miles away, when I caught wind that there was a mother-of-all-sized ritual going to be performed in this offbeat place that I was telling you about and, although it was a lot of whisper and maybe/maybe not stuff, I trekked back there. '*Yes*,' my faithful friends told me, a very Big Man had ordered a super High Mass type production. Could I see it? 'Well, we love you like a brother and you are almost one of us so perhaps, but it is a secret of a positively military grade,' and so on. That night they got really worked up and there was a special sort of frenzy and it was all very ritualistic and unintelligible, only more intense than the ones I had seen before. An hour or so before daylight, they brought out a baby and there was a wonderful quiet and the guy in charge took it and held it up. There were a few more special incantations. Then he took a knife and made two small incisions just under either ear of the kid and caught the drops of blood in something and drank it and there were all sorts of approval expressed, like when congregations in more formal services say, 'Amen.' The fellows on either side of me said, 'Come with us,' and I went along and they said I must go now because it was something they really shouldn't have done, letting me stay so long. They wanted to be able to tell the boss that I had only been there for a few hours but had left before this big sacred and ultra secret climactic, blood drinking event. So I left, stumbling around in the pitch dark, down a track that was bad enough in daylight, and I told the whole thing to a man I knew sometime later and he said they kicked me out because the real conclusion was when they cut the child's throat for real after that sort of introductory phase and I said, 'To hell with you,' and he said, 'You think they was going to let you see that, you *outsider!*' So I don't know. Even now I don't know. I suppose religion has been good friends with all sorts of sacrifice, human and animal, forever, so what's new? Washed by the blood of the lamb, as the head people in my organization used to say. Not that they would have held with this pagan stuff, of course. And this inside stuff, it is self preservation. I understand that. And a lifelong habit. They suck it in with their mother's milk."

Sonia looked a bit shaken by the baby story. "They never do anything like that around here. I know that for sure."

"I don't suppose so. But they might bring a load of guns ashore and sell them to a gang leader and he could knock off a dozen or more citizens of all ages, including babies, over time so what's the difference. It's a more modern approach to life and death and survival than getting a few dollars to take one innocent life—if that was what really happened—but not so far away when you really think about it. All aspects of the survival technique as you called it. Everything looks so peaceful and pretty like the ocean that you can just see around that hillside."

The Charity Man gestured out towards the escarpment.

"You see how tranquil it looks, but underneath it is savage and violent and tough creatures survive and that happens in places like this. It's just the same all over. Nobody gives a damn what happens to these people; businesses exploit them, police rough them up, and politicians lie to them so they got to find any way they can to adjust. Let me tell you another little one."

The Charity Man was beginning to sound like he had put a little something with more authority than water in his morning coffee. He sounded suspiciously animated.

"Too heavy," he said. "Let's lighten up. I'll tell you a chicken story."

Mr. James looked more cheerful than ever. He seemed to know the chicken story in advance.

"Right here in this little village, a fellow from Nebraska gets what he figures is real friendly with a guy they call Arnie. Arnie is a chicken farmer. He has about thirty chickens, maybe forty. This Midwestern farmer has like one million or something like that. The guy tells Arnie that rat control is killing him, what with the quantity he has to spread around to stop the rats taking over. Arnie tells him a big secret. He says, 'Sir, I spend just about nothing on rat poison. I buy a bag of cement and it lasts me more than a year. I mix the cement dust with cornmeal and the rats eat it and they get concrete guts when it mixes with the liquid inside them. They just roll over dead. You think gall stones is something bad?' "

Sonia thought she liked this story better than the other one. She was already becoming resigned to The Charity Man's anecdotes ending with the kind of let down that might call for another drink of coffee, or whatever, to cheer him up. *Perhaps that's his technique,* she thought. But at least this one didn't sound like it would conclude with some human tragedy. Dead rats were okay by her.

"The big chicken farmer has never heard anything like that in his life," continued The Charity Man. "*Intestinal masonry*! Rodents turned to stone for a few pennies. His new bosom friend has just handed him a treasure of local knowledge. Then, a little later, Arnie explains how there is some lottery being conducted by the company that sells him baby chickens out of Kingston. His daughter is deep inside the company and she can fix it so that her dad will win but he has to put a good amount on the certain number so that she can arrange for it to pop up or it's not worth her taking this terrible chance. Like about the equivalent of five thousand American dollars and you collect twenty to one. A nice piece of change to split between these two comrades of the chicken and rat information sharing inner circle. Of course one of them is a big time poultry rancher and the other is a simple, son-of-the-soil, straight-shooting peasant with a few hens—but everybody can do with some extra cash. The guy goes and gets the cash on a U.S. credit card and, even when his vacation time is up and he has to go home, nobody knows where the hell Arnie is. They tell the gentleman that Arnie goes off like that from time to time and nobody knows where. Lots of times we think he's not so right here. They tap their heads."

The Charity Man tapped his temple with his index finger and opened his eyes wide.

"Something wrong with the furniture in the upstairs room! And what's this about a daughter? Arnie had a daughter? It's an inside joke, you see."

Sonia shook her head and said, "I know a little about this place. I took a big loss here and, in a way, dreams I once had were ended just over that hill, but the people showed me kindness and, I think, honesty and understanding. They took care of me in the hurricane and

I still come here every year. You just sound a little disappointed and bitter. Perhaps your dreams of doing good got lost and that happened to you. I'm sorry that it did that to you, sir. But it didn't happen to me. It does not have to happen, you see, even if things don't work out perfectly."

"You're probably right, lady," said The Charity Man. "I have been wrong about almost everything that I got mixed up with. I'm not even interested that much in it all anymore."

Mr. James put a glass of clear liquid in front of him and The Charity Man thanked him politely. The smell of the half a tumbler of unadulterated white cane rum wafted toward Sonia in the eight o'clock morning air.

"I'm still interested in this," said The Charity Man. "Mr. James knows what I enjoy. He knows lots of things. He never touches the stuff, you know. Claims it's more dangerous than dynamite. He is a coconut water man. I think he wants to live for a long time. He's the one that gave me that nickname, The Charity Man, you know. I have one for him too. I call him the Stage Manager. He looks after the curtain that they operate and sometimes he lets you have a peek through it and sometimes he doesn't."

"Please don't pay any attention to him Mrs. Carpenter," said Mr. James, addressing himself directly to Sonia in the way one talks around a man who has had a little too much to drink. "You know we have no real secrets around here."

The Charity Man began nodding off in his chair. This is not uncommon among people who drink white rum for breakfast and he had knocked off two tumblers in less than ten minutes.

Sonia turned to Mr. James. "Poor fellow," she said. "He is so disillusioned. All those stories of how he lost faith in the people that he really wanted to help. And his conclusion that some everlasting barrier exists between, for example, a person like me from another country and the men and women of villages like yours. That you all feel that outsiders might import danger in some way. I know better. I feel absolutely at home here. All the time I experience kindness and trust. Don't you think he is just frustrated and bitter? Maybe the alcohol has something to do with it."

"Well, that is how he sees it. He always talked a lot and perhaps people were cautious of telling him things that he would repeat and maybe get them in trouble. But he was—I mean is—a good fellow. That's why I call him The Charity Man. He went all over the place trying to get his projects going and naturally some of them didn't work out. Those are the only ones he talks about."

The Charity Man had woken up with the ease of those who slip in and out of consciousness, distrusting both states and trying to avoid surrendering completely to either.

"Projects that didn't work out?" he said. "Know what I did one time? I got to know about FAD fishing. That means fishing around a thing called a Fish Attracting Device. You make it by connecting a few big sheets of plywood, or something equally substantial, and anchoring it in about a thousand feet of water. Near the edge of a bank or the island shelf. After a while seagrass and barnacles start growing on it then it really works best. But even before that, even when you just have it moored for a short time, fish begin to congregate under it like they would below a drifting log. But a FAD stays where you put it so you can find it day after day. It's like a natural, maintenance-free fish farm."

He coughed significantly and Mr. James, the perfect host, went and got the bottle and a piece of ice for his empty glass. The Charity Man poured himself a drink that ensured he would stay awake for the duration of the story and set the bottle nearby.

"So we got all the stuff and selected this stretch of coast running west from the cape, Shark Cape that is. There's half a dozen inhabited places along there. We put six of the FADs down. Each one was roughly in front of one town after the other. We made sure to pass the information all up and down the line so nobody would run into them. They worked well there because it was just about fished to death on the bottom but the migratory, surface species would hang around for a while instead of just passing through and new ones were always coming along. We went back after a few weeks and it looked fine. There were all sorts of jack fish and sun fish and other stuff like wahoo and small tuna just a few feet under. I never went back to that particular area. Got sent to another territory around that time"

"Did your organization expand on the project?" asked Sonia. "You must have been pleased with that one, at least."

Mr. James said nothing. He had known The Charity Man a long time. He had not heard a completely new story for a long time, just amended versions.

"No, they never did. The police begged them not to. You see what happened was that guys from towns further up and down the coast started taking fish from the FADs in front of other places than the ones nearer to their location when the devices close-by were temporarily fished out. The people who considered the one on their doorstep as theirs began to mount watches on them, determined to stop this poaching—which was how they saw it. After a few people got killed or, as it was reported, went missing, and a boat or two was sunk, the police came and cut all of the mooring lines. They let the FADs drift away. They had to do something before it turned into a real war. Isn't that a scream?"

Just then Michael came up from the beach. Sonia brightened instantly from her distress at listening to The Charity Man's latest sociological lesson as soon as she saw him. She shook back her hair that the morning wind had started to blow across her face.

Michael carried a snook hung from a short line. The line was passed through the gills and out the mouth and he had the loop on the other end over his wrist. The fish would have weighed at least ten pounds. He put the snook down on a piece of paper that Mr. James spread on the table. The morning sun shone on the silver sides of the fish and the still-golden fins. There was a dark, almost black line running from just behind the head, where the razor-edged gill plates ended, all the way to the tail.

Michael said, "Them sometimes call them sea police. Them got that name from the stripe down the side. Like the one on the police uniforms, you see?"

"I love that name," Sonia said. "We were just hearing a police story too. It was very sad."

"It's not particularly sad," said The Charity Man, pouring another eye opener or closer—who could tell. "It's just the way things always seem to go. One time I got a whole van load of lead as a gift from a battery company for some fellows to make sinkers. Know what happened?"

Sonia, who had a history of The Charity Man's yarns to go on by now, said, "They melted them down and made bullet heads with them?"

The Charity Man looked disconcerted. "Did I tell you the story already?"

"I only met you an hour ago. You never told me that one but somehow it just occurred to me."

"Well, I think that *is* what happened. Yes, that's

the way it went, all right."

Michael spoke to Mr. James, "Frankie caught the snook a few minutes ago. He asked me to give it to you. Louis was casting with the net for bait to put in his lobster pots and him give Frankie a few. Frankie put on a live one and floated it out on the stream and this one took it right as it did get to the break in the sand bar. The fresh water is coming out strong now, with the rain last night. You can see shrimps jumping on the top of the water."

"They come in anytime the bar floods open," Mr. James said. "The river water brings them. Tell Frankie thanks. Can you take the fish out back and give it to Auntie? Stop by later and have some, tell Frankie to come by too."

Michael went to the kitchen holding the fresh soon-to-be lunch wrapped in the paper.

Sonia, watching him go, was remembering back to the days when she had started her own project. It had not turned out much better than The Charity Man's efforts in many ways. She had lost more than she could afford on building that whole villa development only to have a hurricane convert it into matchwood. But the adventure was the greatest memory in her life and it held some unexplainable fascination over her. *What do you mean unexplainable?* she thought. *Of course there is a perfect explanation. I just dodge it.*

After the storm, Sonia had been so distressed that she had gone home to Los Angles and asked the paper to let her go back to work in any department where they could use her. She had been frightened that losing almost all the money her husband left would consign her to some state of destitution. She had gone to live in a flat that made it impossible to ever ask any of her previous friends to drop over and have a glass of wine.

The editor stuck her in a special projects section and she got sent all over the place to interview "interesting" characters and she almost began to enjoy it. The only problem was that they were not as interesting to her as the people in the little outpost village where she had been wiped out, but she tried to make them interesting to her readers.

So here she was. On a visit financed with two years scrimped from her earnings and some of the remnants of her inheritance. *How come you turned that into cash when you were leaving?* she asked herself in those midnight moments of honesty. "For freedom," she whispered to the pillow, "but not for foolishness." She had an appointment set for tomorrow to speak to the general manager of the hotel a few miles west of the village. In the old days she had stayed there although now she was always welcome for her brief visits at the James' house.

There was still a chance.

# THE VILLAGE CURTAIN

# THE PROPOSAL

That evening the dark purple, water-laden clouds came spilling off the mountains and rolled over the harbor. Before the rain began, Sonia could smell it coming on the wind and she loved it as she loved all the smells of the island. She was inside the big room with the high ceiling in the James' house and the almost cold air of the land wind worked its way through the shutters. Even without the rain, the night breeze that flowed off the hills was a different element from the warm rush coming off the sea that dominated the day from mid-morning till sunset.

"They had two names in the old days," Mr. James was telling her. "In colonial times the British called the daytime sea breeze The Doctor. It was supposed to cure their ailments from tuberculosis to arthritis. The best thing about it probably was that it helped to blow away the mosquitoes that carried the yellow fever and malaria in the early days. When the late evening came and the air was from the high places, it reminded them of the sort of wind they had left behind in their wet, chilly lands, I suppose so anyway, and they called the night wind The Undertaker."

"Listen," Sonia said. "Here comes the real rain."

That night it poured until a few hours before dawn and the daybreak was gray and still. Both The Doctor and The Undertaker seemed to be taking a rest.

Sonia's appointment was for breakfast. She set off early, walking along the beach because that was her favorite way, but aware that the downpour might have made the stream too deep and wide to cross and she might have to go back and around by the paved road. It was nearly twice the distance and she could only see the sea in glimpses if she went that way.

Before she got to the river, which was barely a trickle in dry times and only deserved that name for brief intervals, she saw Michael and Frankie on the beach. They were ahead of her but they stopped to let her catch up.

Michael had a cast net in two folds slung over his arm and Frankie carried a little wire cage and two wooden spools filled with nylon fishing line. He had a rolled up fabric bag over his shoulder.

"What are you guys up to this morning?" Sonia asked.

"That was a big rain last night," Frankie said. "Snook—like the one you saw yesterday—should be there more now. We going down by the river mouth and see what is there."

When they got to the stream, now upgraded to river status, it was about ten feet wide. Michael carried her across and the water never quite got above mid-thigh. At least not on him. *Well*, thought Sonia, *that's not such a bad sort of start to the day.*

"I'm very early. I'm going to watch you fish for a bit. I've never seen this one. At least I don't think so. I have seen the cast net business, but only when it was catching little sardines. You plan to get something like that big sea police fish you brought up to the house? Wouldn't that tear it?"

"Sometimes you get small ones in it," said Michael, "but them big ones are too smart; them stay too far out. This is just to get the bait. The pinchers—what you call the sardines." He gathered the cast net into two roughly equal sections, holding the central lead weight in his teeth. When he threw the net it looked like he was spreading a sheet as wide as he could. The net opened into an almost perfect circle, eight feet in diameter, as it fanned out over the water and sank in the shallows about six feet out from the beach. The center crown was tethered to his wrist by a cord. Pulling it in closed the bottom line of small weights and made a purse out of the net. It was sparkling with small, trembling, silver fish.

Michael shook some of them into the little cage and tossed it into the sea. He tied a short line to it then anchored the other end to a stone on the sand. He gave two lively ones to Frankie then threw a couple of others as far out as he could. Where one fell there was a swirl, a slight yellow flash, then the surface turned calm as before.

"Snook was waiting for him," said Michael. "That's his fin that you see when him turns." Sonia remembered the golden fins.

By now, Frankie had a live bait on each line, the hook through the bottom lip of the sardine—or whatever it was properly called. "That way it no trouble him," said Frankie. "He can swim good with it like that."

Sonia thought, *I've seen lots of people back home with metal through their lips and other places and it didn't seem to bother them either.* "That line looks awful thin to catch a fish like you got yesterday."

"You must use light line. If it's heavy it make the baitfish swim unnatural. The snook will know something wrong. Them not so fool, you know. Them have sense. Them no have to read and write to know when something is wrong. You think them want to die?"

The current of the river took the line out quickly, Frankie feeding it smoothly off the spool as it went. Michael put down the net and took the other line. Neither offered Sonia a chance to see if she could catch one. This fine line fishing was obviously not for a novice.

By the time she had to go to her appointment, the two men had six snook on the beach but none of them was as big as the one yesterday. Each time they hooked or lost one Michael would take a fresh bait from the little wire cage. He never had to throw the net again. There was plenty in there.

"What's the bag for?" Sonia asked.

"When we finish here we going up along the flat part beside the river where you always see all them crab holes. Rain like last night fills up the holes and them no can stay down in them. We catch them in the grass and all over the place—even in the trees. Them can climb good if they want. Them have legs to spare."

She left them at their work and walked to the hotel. There was a little watery sunshine now and a promise of brightness in the young day. When she got to the paved path that led to the outside breakfast patio she put on her sandals. She never wore shoes on the beach although people had said that there was always the possibility of cuts from sharp splinters of broken coral washed ashore or even glass but she took the chance in exchange for the sensuous feel of the sand. It meant a lot to her.

"Sonia, it's a fine idea," said the hotel manager. He had known her from the failed development project days. "We have considered it lots of times but we kind of held back. Not sure who would run it and so on. But if you want to put up the money you can have the concession. I can do business with you. I have had little problems with the guys around here from time to time. They don't always do what you expect."

*The Charity Man's doctrine again, I guess.* "Well

I'll get back to you on it, Leslie," she promised him. "You think about thirty to thirty-five feet would do? I looked into the prices and I don't think I can manage a boat much bigger than that. At least not one that looks like you could count on it."

"Try and get it nearer to thirty-five. Some days it chops up quite a bit and you want the guests to feel confident. It looks bad if you get a charter and have to say it's too rough. Better to let them call it short if they feel queasy. They'll be okay about that, maybe a little embarrassed, but they won't go around saying we have a boat that can't go out unless it's calm. Where I worked before we had one so I got a little feel for the marketing side of the party boat business."

"I'll get back to you," Sonia repeated. "I have one more part of it that I have to check out but I wanted to hear from you first."

By the time she got back to the already shrinking river, Michael and Frankie were back on the beach from their crab hunt. The bag was tied and bulged satisfactorily. Frankie was sitting on a rock smoking a ganja cigarette and Michael was cleaning the last of the snook. There were fourteen of them and one that would go a pound or two more than yesterday's specimen. Frankie pointed at the bag.

"Is funny how those crabs stay still when them is packed in the bag but if you touch the outside them gets all vexed and they start pushing them one another around." Frankie poked the bag with a stick and the cracking sound and bulging started. "See how they go on? One night me was taking about twenty bags of them to town after we went catching them at night. You catch them more plenty at night. It was about one in the morning and the van we was in got stopped in a police road block. It was town police from Kingston. Drug patrol or something. Strangers, you know. Police with big guns. Our van had a covered back. One of the officers stuck him flashlight in and said, 'We catch you with a load. That's bags of weed all right. You all going to jail.' Him put his hand in and grabbed the bag at the back and when he pulled it the top came open and the crabs was all over him and the van floor and dropping onto the road. Me ask him who was going to pay for the crabs that we lost and he said, 'Get out of here, you stinking fisherman, before we shoot the whole lot of you.' So we left. He looked like he would do it too."

Sonia threw her head back and laughed.

"For true," Michael said. "Me was there the night. Jimmy that runs the bar was driving and the guy Allan that died was with us."

Frankie finished his smoke and picked up the bag. "Me got to get these up to Auntie's. She have to boil them before the vendor gets here."

As soon as Frankie went on across the river Sonia said, "I want to talk to you, Mike." Michael finished washing the last of the cleaned fish and began stringing them up on two cords. "I have something to put to you." She was trying to hold his gaze, watching to see if she was making a mistake. "I want to try something. I want to get a used yacht and see if we—I—can make a little business out of it. Leslie at the hotel likes the idea. But I won't touch it if you can't be my captain. I see how even the older men of the village know that you have special, natural skill with any boat. I'll split everything with you after the fuel cost and what you have to pay someone to go on the trips with you and things like bait and so on. How does that sound to you?"

Michael hung the two strings with the fish over a sea grape tree branch. "It sounds all right, really. Me will tell you a little later. Just let me think about it for a time. And me got to ask Mr. James, you know. Me sort of work for him now. Here and there."

The sun was out properly now and the friendly wind they used to call The Doctor was all around them. The dark clouds with their oceans of contained tears had been pushed far back over the interior. They were still there in the background but it was easy to ignore them.

The next morning Michael was at the river when Sonia came along the beach on her ritual morning walk. There had been no rain that night and the river had reverted to normal, stream class. The heavier flow of the previous two days had opened the small sand barrier that formed across the outflow and diverted the fresh water to one side in times when the current was light. The breach had not yet healed so there was still a chance of early morning predators congregating to see what was available. Michael had two lines drifted out and looped around sticks in the sand. He did not look particularly optimistic.

He never took any beach fishing seriously. It was a pastime. Sonia was never quite sure what Michael took seriously. *Maybe he takes his position as an eventual sort of successor to Mr. James seriously*, she thought, *but I do not believe he ever thinks about it that way.*

Michael had talked to Mr. James the night before. The old man never gave you hard advice about personal matters. He only issued what sounded like orders when it came to matters that he felt concerned the whole community. He had said just one thing that worried

Michael. He said, "You sure it's only the boat she's buying, Mikey?" When Michael had asked what he meant, Mr. James only smiled and said it was a joke. "Try it if you want, Mikey. It's not like you're going abroad. Just a few miles down the beach. When you go out to the edge and help Frankie with the traps it's further away. Of course you don't get mixed up with outsiders out there. Sharks, maybe, but them is easy to handle."

So he told her he would do it, but asked where she was going to get the boat. She told him that while she was going all over the country interviewing what were supposed to be "interesting" people they had sent her to Miami to meet with some sort of retired spymaster or secret agent who now owned a marina where there were lots of cheap yachts. He got to store them because he knew the right people. These were mostly seized boats and, when the cases were finally disposed, they would be sold at auction and were usually very good deals. He said that "special" sales could be made even before auction as long as the actual cases were closed and the boats withdrawn from public offering and sold by private treaty.

"We could go there and find just the perfect one." She was trying to keep her enthusiasm under reasonable control. "Then you could sail her back down here through the Bahamas. How does that sound?"

"Listen Sonia," Michael said, "Me got to tell you something. Me never told you this before because it didn't matter. Years ago me got into trouble with some drug business and them put me in jail in Miami. Them ain't never going to give me a visa to go up there again."

She could hardly believe it. Not that it had happened, that was easy to understand, and it didn't matter to her any way. What shocked her was that they had been together every day and, later on, plenty nights too, when she had been living here building the villas that the ocean devoured, and he had never once mentioned anything about what must have been a big event in his life. *The curtain*, she thought. *The Charity Man's curtain. Nonsense*, the other voice in her heart said, *anyone might be shy about going to prison. People keep all sorts of things quiet. You do it yourself.*

"Don't worry about it Mike," she said, "I got to know this guy that owns the marina. He'll give me good advice and I'll get him to take the boat over to Nassau or find someone to do that for me. You don't need a visa to go there and then we can bring it down the rest of the way. There's not going to be any problem at all."

"Yes that could work. Me know the Bahamas okay. It wasn't just the one time me went up that way. Know how me got caught? Me used to take small loads, you know. But after a while somebody got to notice and one of the bigger Cuban operators squeezed the guy who used to buy my stuff and told him that he either stopped me or them would put a permanent stop to him. So him turned me in to the cops. Sold me to get himself some big friends. Me wonder where those big friends are now?"

Sonia looked at Michael and saw something that was new to her. She saw that there were some things he could take seriously.

# THE VILLAGE CURTAIN

# CARLOS

"It's thirty-eight feet and it's not fast. Single diesel engine. That's why you can get such a good price. Everybody wants speed nowadays. But it's very economical and comfortable in almost any sea. The whole idea was for long distance cruising and it has a top-of-the-line autopilot—a Robertson. With full tanks it has four hundred miles range. Of course you don't need that for charter fishing but it means that your fuel bill is low. You only need to put a little fuel in her for your day trips and that keeps the weight down."

Carlos, the one-time man of mystery and now marina manager, had been happy to see her again. He had said he always loved to meet people living in unusual places. He said it was like old times. "The Caribbean was my stomping ground Sonia. Lots of fun and games down there—keeping America's backyard free of weeds. All sorts of characters. Fascinating arena. Constant challenge separating the sheep from the goats."

"I want to ask you one other thing." Sonia had thought about this but finally decided that that there was no harm in bringing it up. "I have a friend in Jamaica who is going to run the boat for me. In the past he made a mistake and got involved in a drug bust and they detained him then deported him. Honestly, he's a model citizen now. Do you think you might know anyone from your old circle that might get that forgiven so that—at least some time in the future—he could get permission to come to the States? It might mean a lot to me one day. I understand there are waivers that can be obtained." She wondered how Michael would have liked to hear himself described as a "model citizen."

"Well, leave it with me. I will make a few quiet

enquires. I can't promise you anything because I am not really in the loop exactly but you never quite retire from the sort of game I was in. Don't hold your breath, but if I ever get anywhere with it I'll let you know."

She felt almost as good about it as she had about finding the right boat. Everybody had told her that this man knew all the right people.

Back in Jamaica, they gave her a room at the hotel where she was able to look out the window and see *Osprey* at the dock. She had never really been a boat person before. Her husband had suffered from motion sickness even in cars so that had been part of it. Now, at forty, she had suddenly found that she loved everything about it and would go along on charters and work, truly work, in the cockpit when it got lively. She learned to gaff fish and pin bait, and was beginning to anticipate what to do before Michael had time to say it. That was really important and offset the problem that there was hardly any money in the business.

Almost a year into the operation and she had been pulling down on the precious little reserves which she had left to keep going. More than one of her old acquaintances at home had told her that charter boats with good captains made plenty of money in America. Here it was very intermittent and Michael still spent most of his time doing things for Mr. James. Apparently these also meant nights spent in the mountains. It was quietly left clear that these were private matters. It was a wonderful partnership but far from complete. She wondered, *Would I have tolerated it in the past?* But she didn't know what her husband had done all day back then. If he said he had to go to Denver or New York she figured it was okay. And she was *married* to him. This place is so small and intimate she thought that she would just automatically get included in everything, but it never seemed to work out exactly that way.

More than once she had asked about going up to the little cabin where they had sheltered during the big hurricane and it had always been impossible for some

214

reason or another. She never really pressed the issue because she felt slightly awkward at the idea of hobnobbing with Eva, whom seemed to go back a long way with Michael. *Eva*, she thought, *Eva of the mountain retreat, the quintessential insider.*

Her phone rang. It was Leslie, the hotel manager. "Visitors," he said. "Friends of yours I think. Out on the patio."

There were three of them. One was the man who had sold her the *Osprey* in Miami. He stood up as she came up the steps to the open deck. As square and neat looking as ever with his permanent, thin lipped smile and his rimless glasses.

"Well, Carlos. Of all the people. Come down to see if the boat is okay? See her there."

"Hi Sonia. Meet my two friends. Andy and Bill. A and B I call them. Old friends. Well, young old friends, as you see. Andy is a Haitian."

Andy was very courteous. He actually made a small bow. Bill managed a smile.

215

"How is your little project going, Sonia?" asked Carlos.

"Okay I suppose. We could do with some extra work. Do you want to go fishing?"

"Not quite. But we might have a job for you. Do you think your boat would be available for a special, private, patriotic little job? I mention it because it would perhaps obtain the little favor you asked me for when we last met. If you trust your captain to do this small, confidential job for my friends here, I believe I could almost promise you he would get the waiver you said he needed. Payment for the job would be separate, of course. I would see that my friends paid you in advance. Enough that you could relax for a bit. Not have to live on savings, as they say."

"I'm not living on savings," Sonia said defensively. "What do you mean?"

"Nothing, Sonia. Just a figure of speech. Still, you did say you could do with extra work."

"Sure. But that's a different thing. What is the

job?"

Andy said, "It involves the collection of a compatriot of mine. He has done a lot of very important work for us but the situation has suddenly become very dangerous for him. It is necessary for me to extract him quietly and unofficially and bring him to safety. The matter is delicate. I can still communicate with him and he will be waiting where we tell him but time is not on our side. I will pay you thirty thousand American dollars to do this thing for us. In advance.  It is more than the boat even cost, I believe. And Ben and I will go along. We are useful aboard. This is important because we do not wish anyone else to be involved. I understand that you have complete confidence in your captain?" He spoke as one who understands a lot.

"Are these some of the right people you know, Carlos?" Sonia asked.

"Of course Sonia. That's why I promise you the other little favor."

*He reminds me of Mr. James*, thought Sonia.

*Confident and reasonable, the sort of person who has control over events.* "I will speak to my captain. It is up to him. Do you want to meet him yourself?"

"Oh no," said Carlos. "If he agrees, you will present Andy and Bill to him precisely on departure from here. These are very private people. Tell your captain that the place where he will pick up Andy's unfortunate colleague is near Pointe des Aigrettes to the southeast of Pointe Tiburon. He will be expertly piloted in because Andy knows the place well in the day or the night." He smiled and said, "Perhaps your captain knows the area himself. It is almost the nearest point that Haiti approaches Jamaica."

Sonia put the whole proposal to Michael. The only part she kept to herself was the opportunity to get the travel ban lifted. Not because she did not think they would get it, she just was not quite sure how it might sound and how much it would mean to him. She presented Carlos' plan as if it was a sort of adventure because she thought that would appeal to him. It was less attractive to her than the visa but she had come to know Michael had an affinity to challenges. He always liked to test his own skill. And, of course, there was the money.

He hardly hesitated. "Tell them we can go tomorrow night," he said. "Me got to fill her up and put the little life boat on her. It's a long way. Me can get the diesel fuel first thing in the morning. Then me got to go straighten some things out and we can leave about midnight tomorrow. One thing. Keep them off the boat till we are going. And tell them me no want no gun aboard. Them got to agree to that."

When Sonia told friendly Andy all that he said, "Of course. That is very reasonable. We are not going to invade the country. We are going on a mission of mercy. Only it is of importance that we have communication equipment. We will show these equipments to the captain. You see, we will deliver ourselves and my endangered friend to a government vessel once we are well into international waters. Your captain will be able to run the boat home alone with comfort. It will be sixty miles or less to the east end of Jamaica. Carlos told us you have an autopilot aboard. Does it work well?"

"I think so. We don't use it much but he turns it on sometimes to check it."

"Carlos said to tell you it was wonderful seeing you again. He had to leave this morning. He said you must not worry about anything."

# THE TECHNICAL MEN

Michael opened the sliding door that separated the open back of the boat from the steering station and the forward cabin. Andy and Bill stepped down from the dock, each had a duffel bag and they put them down on the cabin floor. In the bigger bag there were two boxes with hinged lids. Bill opened the boxes and showed Michael some black modules, they had labels on them with various specifications. He explained that they were power supplies for the briefcase-size special phones that were packed as well. Little wire harnesses with plugs were in plastic envelopes. He had two other smaller types of more conventional looking handheld radios or phones.

"Everything is backed up, Captain. Two of everything. Today we use these instead of weapons. They are safe and legal and much more effective. Primitive people shoot it out. Technical people know where to go and when, so there is no shooting. Danger is for people who lack technique."

"So you is always safe?" Michael asked. "Suppose me is some murderer and robber? You going in my boat."

"Ah, but Captain—look at how we do business. We pay you in advance so there is no incentive to cheat us. Your partner is well known. Reputable. We do not charter some boat from a criminal. We reveal everything to you. Even now, if you are uncomfortable, tell us. We call it off. No kind of force is employed. At any level. We are embarked on an errand of mercy to save a man's life. Did not the lady explain that to you?" Andy had taken over the conversation in his friendly way. He looked at Sonia standing on the dock.

"Forget it," Michael said. "Me no mean nothing. Let's go. Put your stuff up front. Show me on the chart exactly where we going to. Then draw it bigger for me on a piece of paper. Me hear you know the place good?"

"Absolutely. I have been in there before. It is not very difficult. In the day, very easy, but even at night not hard. Only it is necessary to stay always on the west side of the harbor. Then you come around to starboard and you can go right to the beach. Sand all the way in. Soft sand. A man can walk right out to the back of a boat like this and you can open the transom door and he can climb in. To go in, get him, and come out—twenty minutes is enough. Thirty at the most. We will not enter till I am sure he is there and ready. Always we shall do everything without danger. With technique." He smiled at Michael. "You are a man of technique too. I sense it. I am very sensitive. Perhaps it is my French background."

Sonia took the mooring lines from Michael and coiled them up on the dock. It was ten minutes after midnight when she could not see the running lights any more. She thought of going to the high ridge near the lighthouse where she could see the boat a long way out but decided against it. Lots of people said it was a bad-luck place.

Bill put the small phone-like radio to his ear, nodded to Andy, and said, "He is ready." There was just a little moonlight and the land had the burnt smell that all of the southwest coast of Haiti has except when it was actually raining. Michael only glanced occasionally at the sketch as he went in. The water in the little bay was shiny and calm. The natural channel was clear white sand and the dark rocky heads were all over on one side. Even in the night the light from the young moon was adequate. Andy stood at his shoulder but never spoke. That is the sign of a good mate—even if he knows the way perfectly. He keeps quiet unless he feels there is something useful to say. Michael could figure the depth with his eyes as well as any depth indicator and saw where the bend in the entrance was with plenty of time to spare. Once past the curve he could see the gently shelving approach, the few patches of grass. Closer in, the grass ended completely and it was pure coral sand. On the beach, two men were visible beside one of the larger of the stunted, twisted trees. He brought her bow around to the south and the back of the boat stopped about fifteen feet from the shore.

Andy opened the door in the transom and dropped the little three-rung boarding ladder. The men on the beach embraced and one came wading out. Michael just touched the engine in reverse and the boat inched back. When the man got to the ladder the water was only midway up his chest. Andy put his hand out and the man grasped it and came aboard. He spoke to Andy in Haitian Creole. He was dripping all over the deck and Andy gave him some dry clothes as Michael took the boat back out through the channel. Andy did not even bother to go back to his post near the wheel. He knew by now that Michael was as good as they came.

"Just put her on 270 degrees as soon as you can clear the most southern point, Captain," Andy said softly. "I will make them come to us. It is easier for them. Bill has spoken to them already and there will be no problem with such good weather. You have done a wonderful job this night and look at this man. He owes his life to you. He does not speak very much English but he requests that I thank you. He was a man with great resources but became exposed for all his good work. Now we make our account square with him. Now we will look after him. He has been a good friend to us and we look after friends. You saw the man with him on the land? He will also spread the word among our people that we save our friends. You are now a friend. You too will be looked after if necessary."

Michael listened to him and thought that he sounded like a man reacting to relief. Relief that his operation had gone smoothly. Many people tend to talk a lot when they relax suddenly.

Bill said, "Okay you love birds. Have a good cruise. I'm going up front to lie down. I'm tired. Should I use any particular bunk Captain?"

"No," said Michael. "Suit yourself. Take the side you like."

"Can I shut the cabin door? It cuts the noise down."

"Anything you like. Make yourself at home." Michael put the autopilot on and matched the course it held to the compass a few times. It had worked fine coming over but he had never had a boat with one before and still could hardly believe the magic of it. It was like having a helmsman on board that never got tired.

There were still a few hours left before daybreak. Michael had the normal running lights on now but, when he saw the other boat coming up on them, there was no illumination on her at all. Just the black bulk of her hull against the lighter background. Bill got up and said, "They will stop, Captain. When it is convenient, come along on her port side. They will put some light on where the ladder is and I will go up and then Andy will follow our friend up. Then you are finished with us. Thank you for your work."

The wind was very light but there was the ever-present Windward Passage swell so, even in the lee of the

227

bigger vessel, everyone had to be alert to the rolling movement. Michael inched up alongside. Bill took a phone that he had not used before and dialed a number into it. He did not speak into the phone. He just looked at the dial and put it back in his pocket. When he saw Michael watching him, he raised his eyebrows in an expression that seemed to say *more technology*. Bill went up, then the refugee, with one last look of relief at Michael. Andy grabbed the rope ladder immediately behind him. There was a pool of light now on the deck of the big gray boat and Michael let the connecting line go the moment the last two men were on the ladder. He put the clutch in and looked back to make sure the stern swung clear of the side of the other vessel. He took one good look back at where the man he had picked up had just reached the top of the boarding ladder.

A square man with rimless glasses, glinting in the light, was standing back from the gunwale. The Haitian stood on the deck and suddenly seemed to crumple. Michael only saw it fleetingly but it looked wrong to him.

He put the boat in neutral to try getting another take on the little scene but the light was off and the gray boat was swinging away and he could hear her powerful engines come to life and that was the end of that.

Michael was thinking as fast as he could. He was trying to think clearly against the natural pressure that his instinct was building. *There's something wrong with it. Me no know what it is and maybe it has nothing to do with me. But me know there's something not right about it. Be reasonable. Try and think clearly without being stupid. What was that technical freak doing with that phone when him was getting off? What kind of phone was that anyway that you only dial and no speak into? Think carefully. The bags. The one who called himself Bill had both of the bags over his shoulder. How come they were so light him could do that?*

The autopilot was holding her steady and Michael corrected the course for Morant Point. He went into the cabin and turned on the two lights. Everything looked fine. He took the thin mattresses off the two bunks, and then he lifted the hatch under the port bunk and saw it instantly. *That's why he shut the door when he went to lie down—the bastard.*

The two black boxes, the alleged "power supplies," were wedged in the corner of the bottom of the storage area and another phone-like object was plugged into the two of them with little wire cables. There was nothing he could see, no dial or any sound, but he knew that only made it worse. He didn't know anything about it but he knew that if he just cut the wires that might be as bad as sitting there watching it. He ran back to the steering station and got out on the side and made it to the front of the boat. He cut the lines holding the lifeboat where it was tied across the bow cap. It had blocked access to the bow from the cabin because it covered the forward hatch. He cut the anchor free from the line and tied the rope to the bow of the lifeboat and pushed the little craft over the side. It trailed behind, bobbing in the straight wake that the autopilot made, tethered by the anchor line.

Michael got back into the stern and tied the tow line to a cleat. He was still trying to think ahead. He knocked the location pins out of the pipe frame that supported the aft canvas canopy, pulled the lifeboat in close, and threw the canopy into it. He cracked off the plastic bracket that held the six inch compass in its location immediately in front of the wheel and took it with him. Then he slipped over the side and, crouching in the little boat, let out the towing line till he was at least fifty feet behind *Osprey*.

*Now let's see what it means. Perhaps it's just some sort of high-tech location thing but me no believe it. Me know there is something wrong. Like that poor idiot did know it when him got on the deck. Him looked like him saw his own ghost or something.*

Michael let out some more line. He felt better when the space was greater.

*Me know something is wrong. Like fish know when a net is around them and it only just restricts them, but them know. Them no have to know how to read and write to feel the danger. Me never brought any water. Me can maybe go back and get a few bottles.*

He started to pull on the rope to close up the distance.

*How could me not take some water? That's stupid. It's right in the stern.*

He was just about twenty feet from the transom, still pulling the boat up to get the water, when the whole front of *Osprey* blew off. Pieces of the boat rained all around him. He cut the line so that the wreckage couldn't pull him down and the small boat drifted clear. In spite of everything, the first thought he had was how his old friend Leo, the dynamiter, would have been impressed. Thinking of Leo, he smiled in the darkness. *What a lesson! Now it is just hard but not impossible.*

*The east wind is my friend. Him live out here all the time. And it is the month of April when the line squalls travel with the wind bringing rain so water is possible too. Anything is possible if you only stay calm.* That was why he had taken the canopy. In the daylight he would cut the canvas from the frame and make some sort of sail from it with the pipe for a mast. He put the compass in the bow and lined it up as best as he could with the center line. The morning star was up now and the very first fingers of gray were spreading out below it. In the daylight he would start to rig the sail with what rope he still had and the canvas straps from the canopy.

*If me let a little more time go by it would have been all over. Me did see how neatly it had been set up. The charge was right under where the lifeboat was tied on top of the bow. And the whole forward bulkhead must have come right back through where the steering wheel was. Them would have got me both ways. Technique all right. Now let's see what the old techniques can do. People sailed for a long time before them ever invented that word.*

He was thinking quite differently now. All the panic was gone and he had plenty of time. All he had to do was keep cool. There was no shortage of water around here and even though it was the kind he couldn't drink it could help him keep cool. He was only waiting for the sun to start working. The first thing was to rig the canvas, and then he would get the top off the center seat and make something that would function as a rudder. The little paddle that was clipped into the lifeboat was too small but if he could tie the seat to it that might be better to steer with.

He went on planning while he watched the daybreak. There is no time of day when the weather gives you more information. He saw the line of dawn clouds with their tops just slanted slightly and the straight, flat bottoms as they lined up along the horizon. *Steady, moderate wind from the east.* Winds that had borne the commerce of the old world and all that came with it. That is why they called them the trade winds. Perhaps the cargo on the slave ships had other names for them. When they came blowing ashore Mr. James had said the English called them The Doctor. Out this far, chilly land wind never affected you. *No Undertaker out here. No Undertaker for me out here.*

During the day he saw a helicopter patrolling. He dropped the little makeshift sail and went over the side and stayed under the shelter of the boat with just enough room in the shadow of the stern to breathe. The chopper flew in very wide circles and finally saw the little boat. It flew low overhead but seemed satisfied that it was nothing interesting and headed off to the north, in the general direction of Guantanamo Bay. He was finished with trusting anything.

# THE VILLAGE CURTAIN

# THE FINAL CURTAIN

"Look out yonder, Cap," said the man in the bow. They were fishermen out of the town of Manchioneal on the northeast coast of Jamaica and were setting deep lines off the north end of the Albatross bank. The boat had the homeport numbers painted on the bow as required on all commercial craft.

Each line was dropped in depths from nine hundred to twelve hundred feet. They had a ten pound sinker and a string of fourteen baited hooks on the end of each one. When they had them down a big balloon buoy was clipped to the line and they left it and went to set another. The normal way was to put down four of them and then come back and pull the first one. If you found that a particular piece of ground was producing better than the other then you bunched them up, concentrating on that area. If results were poor you kept spreading them out, probing blindly for good bottom. It was a tough job pulling up that length of nylon line each time by hand but anything you got at those depths was high grade stuff. Deep water snappers and big groupers, which commanded good prices. What the vendors called "quality fish."

This boat had just put down their last line of the group of four and were back-tracking, looking out for the other buoys and hoping the current hadn't pulled any of them so deep in the water that it made the float hard to see. The current was flowing strongly from east to west. The man running the motor stood up, bracing the tiller arm of the outboard engine hard against his leg to steady it. "Look out there," he said, "It look like a little tree or a log with a big branch on it. Way out in the open like that it must have fish round it." He took up a heavy hand line.

A big log this far out, with the possible accumulation of fish around it, could make your day.

The man in the bow was famous for his eyesight. "It's not a log, Cap," he said. "It's something else." He could see it better all the time as they headed straight toward it. "It's a little boat with some funny piece of sail. Me never seen nothing like it."

The Manchioneal boat came up and Michael knew it was going to be all right now. It had rained the night before and he had caught a little water before the squall moved away so it could have been worse. He had seen quite a few ships heading up and down the passage but he guessed they were more likely to run over him than alter course to look at something so insignificant. The wind had stayed gentle except for when the squall went over him. He could not hold anything even near to a straight course but he did his best and the current was his friend too. He knew that and how lucky he had been that it was going along with the wind in roughly the way he wanted.

"What you doing out here, brother?" said the man

in the front of the boat from Manchioneal. Both of the men were standing up now looking at Michael.

"Do something for me," Michael said. "Give me some water. Me did see one of your markers over there. Go on and fish them. Me okay. Me all right for true. Me can just drift here till you decide to go in. Better you take me in after dark anyway. When you get round the north side of the point put me ashore anywhere. Anywhere not too far from a road. This little boat is yours for the trouble. You found it drifting so you have no problem to explain it. Me no ask you to buy it or anything like that. Take it. But if you can give me a few dollars it would help me a lot so that me can get on any bus or taxi that me find. You no have to worry about nothing. Me know Mr. Hawking—Daddy—from your town and, if you like, you can tell him you picked up a friend of Mr. James from down the west. Better that you no say anything at all but if you want you can tell him. Only him. Him will tell you that you can relax. Me can keep my mouth shut."

The man in the bow gave Michael a plastic bottle

of water and a bag with a few crackers in it. They had a tin of corned beef and half a loaf of bread in the boat as well, but they figured that the lifeboat was not worth a great deal and, if they were going to give this drifter a few dollars for bus fare, then there was no point in missing lunch. It takes a lot of energy to draw up those thousand foot long lines by hand. They were practical men and times were hard.

Michael walked up the familiar gentle incline across the clearing, climbed the few worn steps to the little house and made it to the bed. The weariness engulfed him and he slept truly, in the safety and comfort of being under a sound roof. After a long time he dreamt of the beach and the little river that came and went with the rain and Eva was walking up to him across the warm sand. Sometimes there *is* scent in a dream.

She was sitting on the floor beside the bed and had tried to wake him but not too hard. Jimmy had told her that he was at the cabin in the mountains. She had been visiting Mr. James' wife, whom everyone called Auntie. Jimmy had said, "Me took him up there and now me come for you."

On the way up the hill, Jimmy had asked her how long it would be before the baby and she said that Auntie believed not more that a week. After she got to the little house she did not plan on leaving till afterwards. Auntie was coming to stay with her tomorrow. Auntie was very confident that there would be no problem and, although it was Eva's first, she was very confident too.

"Is he really all right?" she asked Jimmy. "All right for true?"

"Him all right. Me think you going to have him all to yourself for a while. That works out nice for you, eh Eva?"

So she went on sitting there, watching him sleep. The night came on and with it the frequent curtain of evening rain. She thought about starting the Tilley lamp but immediately discarded the idea and just lit a stubby candle, which was in a bottle by the bed. It gave her all

TONY TAME

the light she needed to go on watching over him. She leaned over and held her face just a few inches from his chest for a few minutes, careful not to actually touch him lest he wake. She shut her eyes and thought, *If me ever go blind me will still know when him is near.*

Under the good roof it was a quiet night as the gentle rain went on.


Frankie came up to Sonia who was standing by the little stream on the beach. "Mr. James asked you to come up to the house," he said. He did not go along with her. He went by himself on up toward the flat, grassy, crab country with his bag over his shoulder, walking quickly.

"They found him, Mrs. Carpenter," said Mr. James in his usual formal way. When he spoke to Sonia he phrased his language in the somewhat stilted style that he had learned in the old colonial days at his school, which had still boasted an English headmaster. She noticed the special effort that he made but he always made it.

"Him? You mean the boat?"

"No. Just him. He made it, you know, but he feels that he must be very careful. I agree with him. Your friends—perhaps I should not call them that, but I say it because that is how Leslie at the hotel described them to me—destroyed the boat. I expect they assume they did that to him too. This may protect him. I hope so. I also hope they gave you enough to cover your loss."

Sonia sat down at the old table and knew this was worse than any hurricane. Occasionally, as time had passed, she had thought that this patriarch of the village had looked at her through eyes that seemed quite clear but there was a veil there now.

"I cannot believe it," she said. "I will get in touch with Carlos. He introduced me to those men. They cannot get away with something like that."

"That is up to you but I beg you not to do it. That could be a fatal mistake," said Mr. James. "I believe you will find that some people can get away with anything. It comes from knowing people in the right places, I suppose. But let me suggest that when you go home, as I assume you will do shortly for everyone's sake, but particularly in your own interest, as well as Michael's, understand that you are safe now. If you keep quiet you are simply the victim of an unexpected total loss. Boats are lost all the time. They are stolen, they sink, they catch fire. If it is ever known that Michael is alive then you might be believed to know too much. I tell you this in friendship. So let him be dead for your sake as well. Like the men who tell no tales. Do this favor for us. I considered carefully if I should have even told you that Michael was still alive but I did so out of friendship. Also, I know you were once a newspaper reporter and, if you knew nothing, you may have been tempted to dig. It is what reporters do when they look for answers. So now I ask you, for what remains as friendship, please *do not dig.*"

Sonia looked around at the beach, the peaceful little bay and the few boats that you could see from here anchored in front of the village. Then she looked at Mr.

James and the veil of his eyes. *It's not a veil*, she thought, *it's a curtain. Curtain, hell. It's a wall.*

"Where is he?" she asked.

"Why?"

"I want to give him half the money they gave me. I always promised him that."

"You can give it to me," Mr. James promised her. "I will see that he gets it. He will appreciate that very much in his present situation. Be careful and try to understand. I, myself, do not understand everything completely. There are some things that are beyond me. I am just an old man in a small town. I have enough trouble with little things. A lot of stuff is too big and complicated for me. There are many things that old men and small towns cannot fight but it is possible, sometimes, to hide intelligently and with success. We have been doing it since the days when slavery was supposed to have ended. It must have been even harder then. The old slave masters must have known all the right people."

246

TONY TAME

247

# THE VILLAGE CURTAIN

Photo by Wendy Anne Chinn

# ABOUT THE AUTHOR

Born in 1943, Tony Tame has been associated with the marine industry since the mid 1960's. After 1970 he became directly involved in the supply and service of equipment to the commercial fishing industry in Jamaica. His lifelong interest has been the methods used in various types of fishing and the people who work in this field. Still active in this field his fascination with these topics is undiminished.

# THE VILLAGE CURTAIN

If you enjoyed *The Village Curtain* consider
these other fine Books from
Savant Books and Publications:

*Aloha from Coffee Island* by Walter Miyanari
*Essay, Essay, Essay* by Yasuo Kobachi
*A Whale's Tale* by Daniel S. Janik
*Tropic of California* by R. Page Kaufman

Scheduled for Release in 2009:
*Today I am a Man* by Larry Rodness
*The Bahrain Conspiracy* by Bentley Gates
*The Mythical Voyage* by Robin Ymer
*The Jumper Chronicles: The Quest for Merlin's Map*
by W. C. Peever

If you are an author or prospective author who would like
to be published
contact Savant Books and Publications at
**http://www.savantbooksandpublications.com**

Made in the USA
Charleston, SC
31 December 2009